ever entered Marcus's life ...

nothing more than an extra plate drying in the sink, a wet shower, a rumpled pillow.

And then Marcus saw the gown.

It was hanging over a chair, long and sweet and ... hers.

He knew he hadn't had that gown in the house before she'd come here, and as mad as he could admit to being, he couldn't explain where it had come from.

Unless she had really been here, flesh and blood....

Do you believe in time travel? she'd asked.

He grabbed the gown and brought it up to his face, and tried to imagine the warmth of her body in it.

Slowly he fell to his knees, and for the first time since he could remember, prayed to a God he had almost forgotten, prayed that he wasn't insane, that he hadn't imagined her and that, please God, she would come back to him.

Dear Reader,

Shadows is full of treats for you this month! Terri Herrington's *Flashback* will move you to tears even while it's sending a shiver up your spine and filling your head—and heart—with dreams of a love that can conquer time. Terri's deft touch will make her debut Shadows a book you'll remember for a long, long time.

Evelyn Vaughn is a brand-new author, but she has more than mastered her craft, as you'll discover for yourself when you read *Waiting for the Wolf Moon*. It's hard to believe you can be laughing one minute and quaking with fear the next, but this talented author will make a believer out of you. And in Rand Garner she's created a hero to die for—perhaps literally!

In months to come we'll continue to bring you more wonderful books, each one truly worthy of bearing both the Silhouette and the Shadows names. And I hope that, as time goes by, you'll share your thoughts and feelings about the line with me. I'm always eager to hear from you, because you're the reason we're here, so of course we want to keep you happy.

Meanwhile, happy reading—but don't forget to keep an eye out for whatever might be lurking . . . in the Shadows.

Yours,
Leslie J. Wainger
Senior Editor and Editorial Coordinator

TERRI HERRINGTON

FLASHBACK

SILHOUETTE® Shadows™

Published by Silhouette Books New York

America's Publisher of Contemporary Romance

SILHOUETTE BOOKS
300 East 42nd St., New York, N.Y. 10017

FLASHBACK

Copyright © 1993 by Terri Herrington

ISBN: 0-373-27007-0

First Silhouette Books printing May 1993

Printed in the U.S.A.

TERRI HERRINGTON

lives with her husband and two daughters in Mississippi, but she has lived in eight states and spent part of her childhood in Holland. She feels that falling in love is the most special feeling in the world, one that she experiences each time she writes or reads a romance.

For Ken,
who showed me the relativity of time and love

PROLOGUE

She was gone.

Marcus Stephens stared at the space where she'd sat just moments ago, gazing at him with tragic hope in her eyes, touching his hand with tentative certainty, offering him a precarious balance that he hadn't expected at this point in his life. Then she had slipped through his fingers, disappeared into thin air....

Was she a ghost? he asked himself. Could he have held a ghost the way he'd held her last night? Could she have wept in his arms and clung to him as if she'd spent a lifetime looking for him? Would a ghost have had a fever so violent that he'd had to pack her in ice?

But if not a ghost, then *what* was she...*who* was she... and, more important, *why* was she?

Could it be true, what she had tried to tell him last night? The thing about a camera and crossing lifetimes? No, it couldn't be, he told himself again. She had been hallucinating, babbling. There was no sense to be made of any of it.

She was a blessing that had been sent to divert his attention from the self-destruction he'd been contemplating. Or she was a curse to further punish him for his sins.

Either way, she had been here, and now she was gone. Another secret to hide from the world. Another black spot on the soul he could never cleanse.

But in the throes of his despair, a ray of hope penetrated the blackness in his heart. Maybe she would come back, from whatever black hole she had fallen here from. Maybe he'd get the chance to find out, once and for all, if he was as mad as he thought, or if she really had existed for a moment.

It had been a long time since he'd bowed his head, dropped to his knees and confronted the deity he felt he'd betrayed. As he did it now, he did it with trepidation, humiliation and a great deal of shame. Facing God with his bag of sins was more than he'd been prepared to do, but some burdens were just too heavy to bear alone. The fleeting thought of sharing it with someone who might have been merely a figment of his imagination only made him feel more alone. In just a few hours, she had gotten under his skin, changed something in his life, brought something to him that he'd needed more than air itself. Why couldn't she be real?

He knew why, he thought. It was his term in hell, and he'd earned every one of the searing flames that engulfed his life. Still, if there was even a chance...

This isn't my time. I've traveled back. I'm not making this up, Marcus. You've got to believe me....

What if she hadn't been hallucinating? What if he wasn't mad? What if there was a chance—just a chance—that she had been telling the truth, that she had traveled here through some medium he couldn't understand? What if she could do it again and come back to him?

What if she couldn't?

Dread washed over him, and he felt more dismal than he'd ever felt before. Despair wasn't something that got easier with experience. And this was a trauma he couldn't walk away from.

She had gotten inside him, deep down where he needed her most, and he swore, right there as he knelt on his knees, his head bowed to God, that he would wait as long as it took for her.

He would find her again, even if he had to grow old to do it.

CHAPTER ONE

He was back.

Sarah Rhinehart saw the old, withered man standing in the crowd surrounding her models, and she slowly moved the camera from her face. Unlike the other fans in the mob, who were drooling over the popular faces they'd seen often on television commercials and in magazines, watching every flick of their rich, luscious hair and pressing in to hear their voices as they spoke and laughed, the old man seemed focused on her.

Didn't he know that the photographer was the least interesting person on the set? Didn't he realize that she was at least four inches shorter than most of them, that her hair hadn't been teased and curled and styled by the finest hairdressers in the business, that her body was so small and slender that it seemed childlike next to the world-class beauties she photographed?

She was no draw, she thought, at least not like them, yet he stared at her, his gaze penetrating her concentration as it had done the other half-dozen times she had seen him watching her work. He was following her, she thought with a chill. And each time, he grew closer, bolder, until she wondered what he might do if he reached her.

Tearing her eyes from him, she stepped over to one of the guards holding back the crowd. "John, that old man I told you about—the one who's been following me—that's him, over there."

The guard scanned the crowd until he found the gray head, the slumped body, the sad eyes.

He knew she was talking about him, Sarah thought instantly, for something changed in his stance. Slowly he stood straighter, almost in readiness for some revelation he wasn't prepared to unveil.

"I'll go talk to him," John said. "See if I can find out what his problem is."

Unable to tear her eyes from the old man, she grabbed the guard's sleeve. "Listen, go easy on him. He hasn't done anything threatening. I just need to know why—"

"Why he's stalking you," the guard finished for her. "Don't worry, Sarah. Leave it to me."

John started toward him, and she let out the breath she'd been holding. But as she started to turn back to her models to finish the shoot, she was stopped by the desperate look of betrayal that passed over the old man's face.

I just want to talk to you, a voice from some distant place in her mind cried out. *Just touch you...*

Sarah shuddered as the sensation passed over her, a sensation she'd only felt the few times she and her twin sister had communicated telepathically, knowing things they couldn't have known, feeling things they couldn't have felt, hearing things they couldn't have heard.

He began to back away, still staring at her, and fear made her quell the urge to stop the guard, abandon the shoot and go to the man herself, to dive into the unknown waters to which he seemed to draw her.

Instead, she stood frozen, watching as John called out for him to stop. The old man looked away from her, breaking the powerful spell she'd been cocooned in, and as the crowd split behind him, he turned and fled through the people.

Not like this, Sarah. I didn't want it like this....

The sensation terrorized her again, gripping her with its intensity, and she watched, paralyzed, as John broke into a run, shouting for him to stop, reaching out to grab him.

Traffic whizzed by, not heeding the old man heading for the street. She caught her breath as he picked up speed, looking over his shoulder as he bolted away from the guard, who was catching up to him. She saw his eyes cutting into hers with a passion that cut through every door in her soul and threw them all open wide. A car flew toward him, and his old body slowed with fatigue.

A scream tore from her throat as she heard the deadly sound of metal against bone, saw the look of surprise and then pain on his wizened face, and watched his body hurled through the air to land limp and lifeless on the asphalt as other cars screeched and skidded to a halt.

Dropping her camera, she tore through the crowd, out into the street, and threw herself to her knees beside him. "Call an ambulance!" she heard John yelling, and then someone was grabbing for the old man's wrist, feeling for a pulse. But even as she waited for some sign of life, some explanation, some hint of hope...she knew in her heart that he was dead.

Moments later, as she watched his body being loaded into the quiet, unhurried ambulance, she was confronted with the eerie sense of having lost something vitally important to her. Something she had needed. Something that would have filled the void that had been growing in her soul.

She didn't know where the tears for this man she had never known came from, but inexplicable grief overtook her. Unable to continue with her work, she sent her models and crew home and retreated to the home that was her only sanctuary when those dismal thoughts of "unrightness" chased her into hiding. Curling up on her bed, a bed that had seen many tears, she wept harder than she ever had before.

And this time it was for an old man she had never even met.

The ringing of the telephone cut into a disturbing half dream about reaching for something she couldn't quite grasp, and Sarah sat up and reached for the phone. "Hello?"

"Sarah, it's me. John."

Raking her hand through her hair, she nodded. "Yeah, John. Did you find out anything?"

"His name was Marcus Stephens," the guard said. "He was seventy-five years old. A retired doctor. They're burying him tomorrow."

That grief that had drawn her under its dismal spell welled up inside her again. Now he wasn't just a face.

He had a name and an age and an occupation. "Did—did you find out what he was doing there?"

"No," John said. "I'm sorry, Sarah. I wish you hadn't had to see that whole thing."

She tried to comfort him, to tell him that she was fine, that it was just one of those flukes that no one could explain ... but somehow her voice wouldn't function around the knot forming in her throat.

"I hope to God you aren't blaming yourself."

She let out a deep sigh. "I just wish I knew why he was watching me."

"Why wouldn't he be?" her guard asked softly. "You're not that hard on the eyes, you know. He probably had some perverted old-man crush or something."

"Then why didn't he have it on Cindy or Belle or any of the models? Why me?"

"What can I say?" he asked. "He had better taste than most of the fans."

Sarah managed a soft smile. "Thanks, John. You're real sweet."

"Yeah, well. I gotta go. Are you gonna need me tomorrow?"

"I'll let you know."

She set the phone back in its cradle and dropped back onto the bed. Marcus Stephens. Not the name of an old man at all. It was a sweet, romantic name, a name attached to a person who felt things deeply behind those piercing, sad blue eyes. Who had Marcus Stephens been?

Tears came to her eyes again, and she tried to divert the memory of that body slumped on the street.

Not like this, Sarah. I didn't want it like this. Had that been his voice calling to her subconscious, or just a too-vivid imagination filling in blanks that her mind couldn't fathom?

"Sarah!"

Her sister's voice from the front of the old house made her jump, and she caught her breath and shouted, "Back here, Caren."

Her sister reached the door of her bedroom and, glancing in, said, "Oh, God. They said you took it hard, but you're really falling apart, aren't you?"

Sarah got off the bed and turned away from the face that was identical to hers except for the scar that cut across Caren's eyebrow from where she had fallen when they were three. It wasn't their only difference, however. Caren wore her dark hair short and permed into sweet waves that framed her face and brightened her perky, mischievous eyes. Sarah's brushed her shoulders in one sweeping length, lending dramatic depths to her already thoughtful blue eyes. Their uncle, who had raised them from infancy after their parents were killed in a car crash, used to say Caren was simplicity, sweetness and sensitivity, and Sarah was imagination, passion and restlessness.

"I'm not falling apart," Sarah whispered, going to her mirror and wiping away the smeared mascara from under her eyes. "It's just that it's hard to bounce back after seeing a man get killed in front of you. Especially when you're the reason for it."

"Wrong. I talked to Cindy," she said, referring to one of the models, who had been friends with her since college. "She said you were blaming yourself, which didn't surprise me a bit. It's just like you to think something like that would have anything to do with you."

"Come on, Caren," she said, spinning around. "The man was following me, watching me. He didn't do anything wrong, and I sent John after him. If I hadn't—he wouldn't have run out into the street!"

Caren came up next to Sarah in front of the mirror and set her arm around her shoulders. "It was his time, honey. You can't blame yourself. You couldn't have caused it, and you couldn't have stopped it, either."

Sarah regarded both their faces in the mirror as they leaned their heads together. "It doesn't change the way I feel, Caren," she whispered.

"I know."

"I'm going to his funeral."

Caren got one of those rare lines between her brows and regarded her sister with disapproving eyes. "Any way I could talk you out of it?"

"Afraid not. I have to do it."

"Then I'll go with you."

Sarah smiled. "On a Saturday afternoon? Oh, Caren, I would think a newlywed would have something better to do on a lazy Saturday afternoon than to go to the funeral of an old man she didn't know."

"I would think you would, too."

Sarah released her sister and went back to the bed. "No, it's really my problem, Caren. It's something I have to do, and really, I need to do it alone."

Caren leaned back against the dresser and watched her sister smooth out the spread on her bed. "I love you, you know."

"Yeah, me, too," Sarah whispered. "I'm gonna be all right, sis. Just let me do this."

Caren hesitated, then expelled a weary sigh. "Okay," she said finally. "It's not like I can stop you. Are you absolutely sure you're okay?"

"Absolutely sure," Sarah said. "Now go home to your husband. If I had someone like him waiting for me, I sure wouldn't be hanging around you, looking for something to worry about."

"All right," Caren said, pressing a kiss to her cheek. "Call if you need me." Starting out of the room, she blew a kiss to Sarah.

As they'd always done since they were two years old, Sarah pretended to catch it, then brought her closed hand to her heart. With her other hand, she blew a kiss back.

Caren caught it and, grinning, started through the door. "See you later. Call if you get weird."

"I'm always weird, according to you."

"Yeah, well, call if you get weirder."

As Caren left her alone, Sarah laughed for the first time since the accident.

CHAPTER TWO

There were no more than a handful of people at Marcus Stephens's grave site, and it was apparent from the sparse words the pastor offered in his honor that he didn't know the man for whom he spoke.

The coffin was the most basic offered by the funeral home, and there were only two simple sprays of flowers to lay on his grave. One of those was from her.

Sarah stood reverently in the small circle of people until the service was over, her eyes darting now and then to the plump little woman who cried openly over the grave. She was the only one who shed a tear, and, as if she were the only family member, the others waited with quiet words and soft hugs before returning to their cars.

Sarah waited until they were all gone, then slowly she approached the woman. "I...I'm sorry," she whispered. "I'm Sarah Rhinehart."

The woman didn't seem to recognize the name, but she reached out and drew her into a hug. "I'm Stella Brown," she said in a thick Irish brogue. "Mark's landlady for the past seventeen years, I was. Were you a relative? I've been hopin' for a relative to come get his things, but, poor man that he was, there didn't seem to be any."

The hopeful look in Stella's eyes planted the idea in Sarah's mind, and then it took root as she realized that it was a priceless opportunity to learn more about who he was and why he'd followed her. Suddenly that idea was very important to her, and she whispered, "I was his great-niece ... but I'm afraid I never knew him."

"Oh, my, then you did miss out," Stella said, dabbing at her eyes again. "A wonderful man, he was, with a wonderful heart. Not many knew it, since he kept to himself." She set her hand through Sarah's arm and started back to her little car. "You'll come with me, darlin', and I'll tell you all about him. It'll be like a wake in his honor. He would have liked it, he would."

A pang of guilt edged up inside Sarah, but she couldn't make herself turn away from the invitation that tugged at her. "All right," she said quietly. "I'd love hearing anything you could tell me about him."

Half an hour later, they were sitting in the room where Marcus had boarded in the big old house, and Sarah was looking reverently around at the things that had been his as Stella gathered them into a box. "He would want you to have these, he would," the woman said, sniffing as she organized the box.

A cuckoo clock on the wall sounded three o'clock, and a little Dutch girl glided through two tiny doors and danced in a circle. Stella looked up at it and her eyes filled with tears again. "Oh, my. That's his. I wonder, dear, if you wouldn't mind too much if I ... That is, I'd like to keep the clock. 'Twouldn't be the same in this lonely old house if I couldn't count on that clock marking the hours."

"Of course," Sarah whispered. "Listen, I don't have to take any of this. I don't have any right to it. I just wanted to know things about him. You knew him, and I didn't, and—"

"No, darlin', I can't keep them. You take them and learn him. He was a wonderful man to know." She sat down on the bed and touched Sarah's face. "It's too bad that he never met you. You might have brought some joy into that sad heart of his."

"Sad?" she asked. "Why was he sad?"

Stella's shrug was helpless. "I gave up tryin' to figure it out long ago, but I have my theories, I do. He was a doctor, you know. A well-respected one. But then there was Korea . . ."

"He went to Korea? As a doctor?"

"He was in one of those mobile medical groups...."

"A MASH unit?" Sarah cut in.

"Yes, a MASH unit. Worked there for two years, he did. Never was the same after he came back. Retired from medicine completely and went into research, locked away in a lab all the time. And then there was the woman."

"What woman?"

Stella smiled a conspiratorial smile and leaned closer to Sarah. "The love of his life, she was. Over forty years ago. She was a secret love, though, and it's my guess that she was a married woman, since they were destined to be apart. Never got over her, poor man. I think he loved her until the day he died. It was strange, it was...."

"What was?" Sarah asked on a whisper.

"I always had the feeling that he was waiting for her, as though she would change her mind and come back to him. Oh, I would have sold my soul to find out what kind of woman could inspire such love and loyalty in a man."

"She must have been some woman."

"No doubt." Stella got to her feet and looked around at the neat little room where Marcus had lived for the past seventeen years. "It won't be the same without him. But my heart can't mourn completely. He must be happier now than he was here. Maybe he's found peace at last."

The sky opened up in a torrential downpour as Sarah drove home, matching the storm cloud of grief that was still hanging over her for no logical reason. All the way home, Stella's words played in her mind. *Maybe he's found peace at last.* So why did Sarah have to feel such a lack of peace? Why did something about this stranger's death plague her so intensely?

When she pulled into the gravel driveway of the hundred-year-old house she'd lived in since she'd bought it a year ago, she carried the box into the house and set it down in her favorite room, the room she'd converted into a darkroom.

Kneeling on the floor beside the box, she reached through the various items Stella had packed and pulled out a yellowed snapshot of a man in an army uniform. It was him, probably over four decades ago. Standing on her knees, she reached for the string attached to the light bulb and turned on the light.

Sinking down again, she studied the photograph. He was a striking man, though she wouldn't have called him handsome. His face was strong and commanding. There was pride in his eyes, and a touch of humor that contradicted the sadness Stella had mentioned. By her calculations, this picture had probably been taken before Korea, and probably before the woman had come into his life.

She reached back into the box, found his yellowed medical degree from Tulane University, framed and sandwiched between a Bible, a novel and a book on Einstein.

She heard the front door open, then her sister's voice calling, "Sarah!"

"In here," she shouted. "In the darkroom."

In seconds, the door came open, and Caren stuck her head in. It was wet from darting through the rain, and she pulled her wet clothes away from her body, as if that would make them dry faster. "Just came by to make sure you're all right. How'd the funeral go?"

Sarah didn't move to get up. "Fine. I met his landlady." She drew out a watch that had seen better days, a pair of tarnished cuff links, a comb.

"And?"

"And what?"

"And are you satisfied? Did you put all this to rest?"

Sarah looked up from the box. "Stella gave me his things."

"Who's Stella?"

"His landlady." She pulled a white hair out of the comb and gazed down at it between her fingers. "He was all alone in the world.... It's so sad. There was really no one, so she told me I could have them."

A bolt of thunder struck, shaking the house, as Caren slowly lowered to the floor beside her. "Sarah, I don't think this is healthy. You shouldn't be wallowing in this." She reached for the box. "Come on, let me throw this stuff away."

"No!" Sarah slid the box out of her sister's reach. "I need this, Caren." She felt that familiar, irrational emotion rising to her throat, and her lips began to tremble. "You can't possibly understand. This isn't just curiosity. I need to know what I can about him. I'm responsible for what happened to him."

"No, you're not," Caren said. "He's responsible. When a man stalks a woman, he deserves whatever happens to him."

"He didn't deserve to die," Sarah bit out.

"Sarah, you could have been the victim. It was weird, his following you. Maybe you need counseling or something, to confront this guilt you're feeling, work through it...."

As Caren rambled on about shrinks and codependency and twelve-step programs, Sarah pulled more out of his box. There was a razor and a toothbrush. A pack of Juicy Fruit gum. An envelope with more pictures.

She tore open the envelope and pulled out the first snapshot, and suddenly she didn't hear another word her sister said. There was a woman in the picture, standing arm in arm with Marcus, a woman whose face she knew....

"Sarah, listen to me!" Caren insisted. "An obsession like this..." Her voice faded away when she saw the stunned look on Sarah's face. "Sarah, what's wrong?"

Words wouldn't come, so Sarah just handed the torn, yellowed picture to her sister.

Caren took it and, without recognition, studied the man's face. It wasn't until she looked at the woman that she brought her eyes back to Sarah. "This is you, Sarah," she said. "When did you have this taken? And who's this guy?"

Sarah's eyes were luminous as she took the picture back. "The man is Marcus Stephens. But it isn't me." She took the picture back, studied it, then compared the face again with the snapshot of Marcus alone. "This was taken at least fifteen years before we were even born."

"No way." Caren scooted closer to Sarah and studied the picture over her shoulder. "How do you know?"

"Because this picture was taken in the fifties," she said. "And he's the same age here. Look."

Caren sat back on her heels and studied the photo of the man in uniform. "Wow. This is creepy. She looks just like you. Right down to the hairstyle. Even the clothes. You have a sweater like that, don't you? One of those thrift-shop numbers that keeps you from entering the nineties entirely."

Sarah nodded. "Yeah, but it's not me. This is the weirdest coincidence I've ever seen."

Caren looked at the picture, and when she spoke again, her voice was low. "But it looks just like you."

Sarah shook her head. "It must be a relative of ours or something. Who could it have been?"

"No one on Mom's side of the family looked like us," Caren said. "And there were no aunts or cousins on Dad's side."

"Well, at least it explains one thing," Sarah said quietly.

"What's that?"

"Why he was watching me. Stella said he had a great love years ago. If this is the woman, and she looked this much like me, maybe that was why he was following me."

"Wow, that's kind of sad," Caren said. "You must have reminded him of her."

"Yeah." *I just want to talk to you. Just touch you . . .* That distant voice she could have sworn she'd heard somewhere in the back of her mind played again, and tears came to her eyes. Leaning back against the wall, she closed her eyes. "And I had to send that damn guard chasing after him, for no good reason."

"Why did he run if he wasn't out to get you?"

"Because," Sarah answered, without thinking, "he didn't want us to meet that way. Not with a guard interrogating him, and me suspicious."

Caren gave her a dubious look. "And how on earth could you be so sure?"

"I just am," she said. She brought her eyes back to her sister's, locked them in. "Remember all the times when you and I have just *known* things about each other? Like when you got hurt when we were in the second grade, way at the other end of the school, and

I got up and ran out of class to find you? I just knew...."

Caren smiled. "Or when you were kissed for the first time, and I told Aunt Edith before you'd even gotten home."

"Or when I knew Jimmy had proposed to you before you showed me the ring." She sighed and leaned forward, wanting so badly for Caren to understand. "That's how I know about Marcus," she said. "I got one of those feelings. Heard his voice..."

Caren frowned and gave her a skeptical look. "We're twins, Sarah. None of that stuff is uncommon with twins. But don't you think your imagination is running away with you? I mean, you wouldn't have that kind of connection with some old man you've never met."

Sarah's eyes wandered off, and once again she saw the old man running toward the street, looking desperately back over his shoulder, staring at her as if she played some vital role in his life. "I know what I felt," she whispered.

"And I know what I feel," Caren said, picking up the items Sarah had taken from the box and repacking them. "And my feeling is that you've dwelled on this long enough. I'm taking this stuff home with me."

Sarah lunged for the box, and Caren slid it away, stopping her.

"Listen to me, Sarah. You've found what you needed to know. He was following you because you looked like his old flame. End of story. Now, I'm not going to let you sit around here wallowing in guilt and self-recrimination, or following that rampant imagination of yours down some crazy path. You've got to get over this.''

"I will," Sarah bit out, "but you're not taking that box anywhere. I need it."

Jerking the box back, Sarah put it out of Caren's reach.

"Damn it, Sarah. You're just asking for gloom and doom.''

"I'm just asking to have my private thoughts respected, Caren. I'll handle this my way, okay?''

Caren threw up her hands and got to her feet. "Fine. See if I care. I'll just mind my own business...."

Sarah smirked. "Likely prospect."

"Yeah, well, you wait until the next time you see *me* down and see if you can keep *your* nose out of it."

"Never happen," Sarah said. "You're too happily married. Sickeningly so. You'll never be depressed again, so I guess I'll have to feel it for both of us.''

Caren laughed. "Do I detect a little tiny note of jealousy there?''

"Not jealousy. Envy. I'd like a Mr. Perfect of my own. But everybody I date either turns out to have a prison record, a harem of ex-wives, or a secret boyfriend of his own on the side.''

"So you're going to create a Mr. Perfect out of these pictures and start obsessing about some guy you never even knew?''

Sarah tried to push back the irritation sharpening her voice. "No, Caren. I'm not going to obsess. I have too much work to do. I'm just curious, that's all.''

A drop of water plopped onto her knee, and she looked up to see the wet place on the ceiling. "Darn it, the roof's leaking again."

"You want me to get Jimmy to patch it up for you?"

Sarah smiled. "Yeah. I'm sure he'd like nothing better than to spend a couple of days working on his sister-in-law's roof."

"He wouldn't mind, really. He worries about you, too."

Sarah breathed in a deep sigh. "It's okay. I can afford to hire somebody. I just never think about it except when it's raining."

She pulled herself to her feet and examined the wet spot on her ceiling. "I'm gonna take a bucket up to the attic to catch the leak before it ruins my ceiling."

"Guess I'll go home," Caren said. "Jimmy's probably worried about me in this storm. My luck, the bridge'll flood again and I won't be able to get across." She caught her sister's arm. "You sure I can't convince you to let me have his stuff?"

"Positive," Sarah said. "And stop worrying. Mentally, I'm healthier than anyone I know."

"Yeah. That's why you insist on living in this mausoleum and ignoring the modern conveniences any civilized moron would insist on."

"Just because I don't own a microwave or a television doesn't mean there's something wrong with me. And I love this house. You'll grow to love it, too."

"Lay some mauve carpet, slap up some bright-colored wallpaper, remodel the kitchen, and we'll see."

"I'm keeping it authentic," Sarah said. "Geez, how you and I ever got to be twins with such different tastes is beyond me." She grabbed a bucket from a closet and led her sister out of the darkroom.

Caren stopped at the front door and turned back. "Call me if you change your mind about Jimmy and the roof. Or the other thing."

Sarah waved her off as she started up the stairs.

The attic was dark, but a lone, dusty bulb came on as soon as Sarah flicked the switch at the top of the stairs. It was a small attic, no bigger than the size of a bedroom, but it was filled with junk left from generations of occupants. Someday, she thought, she'd have to come up here and uncover some of the waiting treasures.

But right now she had to catch these leaks.

Though the roof seemed to leak in several places, she found the one that was puddling the most and seeping through her darkroom ceiling. A box next to the puddle had caught some of the spill, and it was soaked through. She tried to move it over, but the old cardboard tore in her hand. Managing to move it anyway, she set the bucket down, made sure it caught the leak, then looked around for something with which to clean up the mess.

An old, yellowed sheet covered an easy chair that someone had left up here long ago, a piece that she doubted had been dragged up here for storage. It was here as furnishing for this room, she thought, wondering who would want to spend time up in the most dismal part of this house.

And yet, as the rain pattered against the roof, she had to admit to feeling some of its appeal.

She grabbed the sheet and mopped up the puddle with it, then glanced back at the chair. It was torn, the stuffing was coming out, and the pattern on its fabric was so faded that in this light she couldn't even tell its color. Still, it looked inviting, and if it hadn't smelled of age and mildew, she might have found comfort in it.

She turned back to the wet box and threw back the flap that she had torn trying to move it. She looked inside at the contents that had gotten wet and retrieved an old black telephone with a rotary dial. She wondered if it still worked.

Beneath it lay an old toaster and, next to it, a camera.

Retrieving them both, she dried them off, then studied the camera. It was a big black box, too bulky for her tastes today, outdated and probably useless. But something about it intrigued her, and she brought the viewfinder to her eye, looked at the chair and wondered what kind of pictures it would take today. Film would be hard to get for it, but if she could order it, it might be an interesting experiment.

She got to her feet and took the camera with her when she went back down to get another bucket and some bowls for the other leaks. But before she did, she pulled out one of her suppliers' catalogs and flipped through it, looking for the film that she thought would fit this old camera. When she found it, she left it open on her desk to remind her to order it first thing Monday morning. Maybe the antiquated look in some of her shoots would interest some of her clients, she thought. One never knew.

She was always willing to see through the eyes of age, as if the past held answers she couldn't fathom today. That was why she'd always loved old things, like this house and the antique furnishings she'd chosen for it.

Even her wardrobe had an antique flavor, for she'd always leaned toward tastes her sister found bizarre. Things like flapper dresses for formal gatherings or strapless dresses with big, full skirts, soft sweaters with baby-doll collars.... Her imagination had always lent itself to the past, as if in those times she might have found more of a sense of simplicity and completeness. That, she supposed, was why Marcus Stephens intrigued her so. That was why she couldn't get him off her mind.

As soon as she'd taken care of the leaks, she found herself gravitating back to the darkroom, where his things still seemed to beckon to her. Sitting on the floor again, she dug down to the bottom of the box and gathered together all the snapshots.

Slowly she began to go through them. There was one of him as a young man with some of his buddies, standing in front of an old Chevrolet, with the words Houston or Bust written on the side. In another he wore a track uniform, standing after a college meet with a trophy in his hand.

She smiled at the laughter in his eyes, the carefree air about him, the youthful exuberance. She wondered if the women had chased after him, even in that prim and proper day when women never called men. She wondered if he'd been a ladies' man in college.

She flipped through them, growing more intrigued with each photograph, each expression, each smile. She saw the pride in his stance as he stood in cap and gown, holding his medical degree from Tulane. There was some quality about him, whether it was in his confident stance or the alertness in his eyes, that made him more handsome the more she studied him.

He was someone she wished she'd known.

She saw a picture of his unit in the army and found him in the group, freshly crew-cut and uniformed. Then there were a few she decided must have been taken in Korea, in front of his MASH unit, him and several others—doctors, nurses, orderlies. But instead of the laughter in his eyes, she noted heart-deep fatigue.

Never was the same after he came back.

Stella's words played through her mind, and she wondered what had faced him there that could have made him forsake medicine, that could have stolen the laughter from his eyes.

The last picture was of him in front of a house, holding a For Sale sign upside down, as if he'd just closed the deal and was about to dispose of the sign. He was laughing, and she studied the photo closely, trying to determine whether it was before or after he'd left for the war. Something about the carefree, playful spirit in his eyes told her it was before.

She looked at the house behind him and the two on either side of his, and something started inside her. There was a strange familiarity, an eerie recognition.

It looked just like her house.

She caught her breath, got to her feet and grabbed the magnifying glass she kept on her workbench. Putting the picture under her bright light, she studied the house. The windows were the same, dormer windows coming out from the roof—three of them—and long oval ones on the front of the house, something rare for that time. Something stirred in some intuitive part of her being as she checked the heavy front door, the steps leading to it, the columns on the porch, the railing surrounding it, the big magnolia tree on the right side of the yard....

It was her house.

An invisible fist seemed to knock the breath out of her, and quickly she tried to find something to invalidate the coincidence. The houses on either side were different....

But her neighbors had bought the property, knocked the houses down and rebuilt. Hers was the oldest house on the block, and while it had been restored, it still looked exactly as it had in the picture.

None of this made sense.

Feeling as if she were smothering under the weight of these discoveries, she slipped the picture into her pocket and went out back, where she kept her bicycle. It had stopped raining, and the sky was awash with fresh sunshine and the hint of a rainbow in the east. She got on her bike and rode down her gravel driveway and down the street, pedaling as fast and hard as she could, as if the sheer physical exertion could clear the confusion from her mind.

The street was bright with rainwash, and a steamy fog floated up from the heat of it. The tin roof on the convenience store just outside her neighborhood reflected a blinding shard of sunlight, and rain dripped from the eaves around the roof over the gas pumps. She pedaled past and on up the hill, where an apartment complex covered the landscape on the right and small children played outside making mud pies.

On the left was an old abandoned church whose history she'd always meant to look into, but never had. It was boarded up and rotting, waiting to be torn down so that the lot could be cleared for a parking lot or a fast-food restaurant or a gas station.

A small bridge loomed up ahead, and beneath it, the rain-swollen Dawn River billowed past. She rode over the bridge and turned up the street that led to her sister's house.

Caren and Jimmy were curled up on the front porch swing, watching the afternoon tick by. Sarah smiled. It was nice seeing her sister so happy, so in communion with someone besides herself. She couldn't help envying it, though, for it hadn't happened for her. The men she went out with lacked whatever it took to win Sarah over. Sarah had begun to think it was some tragic flaw within her, that she didn't have the capacity to love anyone fiercely, deeply, the way Caren obviously loved her husband.

"I'll bet you came to hook me into fixing your roof," Jimmy teased as she parked her bike and came up to join them on the porch.

"Nah. There's such a challenge in trying to catch all the leaks with buckets and bowls. What fun would it be to have a sound roof?"

"You really ought to get that fixed, Sarah," Caren said. "That house cost too much to let it go to pot."

"Don't worry," she said. "I'm getting an estimate this week, as soon as I have time. I have to finish the shoot for the Liz Claiborne ad, and then I have to start work on the next Spiegel catalog. I'll work it in, though."

"If you'd give up your obsession with that man, you might have more time."

Sarah pulled the picture out of her pocket, looked at it again, then sat down in the rocker across from their swing. "I came to show you this." She handed Caren the picture, and Jimmy looked at it over her shoulder.

"Is that the guy who got killed?"

"Yeah," Sarah said. "This picture is from sometime in the fifties, or even before that. And check out that house."

Caren looked up at her sister. "It looks like yours."

"It is mine."

Caren lifted one brow. It was a talent Sarah had never acquired. "Come on, Sarah. This isn't your house. The neighborhood's different."

"The houses on either side of me are new, Caren. You know that. Look at the windows, the doors. Look at the tree, for heaven's sake."

Caren tossed the picture back to her sister. "Coincidence."

Sarah compressed her lips and turned to her brother-in-law. "Come on, Jimmy, you must see the resemblance. Tell her."

"It does look like your house," he said. "But it's not like they threw away the blueprint after they built yours. His was the same as yours. It would be too weird for it to be the same house."

Sarah sat back and let out a heavy sigh. "Everything about this is weird. Caren, did you tell him about the woman in the picture?"

"Yeah," Caren said. "So there are two coincidences. It's why he was intrigued with you, Sarah. Don't make some big Twilight Zone thing out of it."

Sarah shook her head and tried to find words to make them understand. "I can't explain this feeling I have about all this."

"It's called obsessive-compulsive behavior, Sarah. You need a shrink."

"What I need is some documentation," Sarah said, as if she hadn't heard her sister at all. "I'm going to go look through the city's records Monday morning. If he ever owned my house, it'll be a matter of public record."

Caren shot her husband an eloquent look, and he shrugged. "Tell me, Sarah. Are you going to work this in before or after your Liz Claiborne ad, or during your Spiegel shoot?"

"I'll work it in first thing Monday," Sarah said. "I just need to know."

"And if you find out he never lived in your house?"

"Then I'll probably lose interest in all this and get back to my boring, unadventurous routine," Sarah said. "Would that make you happy?"

"Ecstatic," Caren said. "I hate it when you're spacey."

"And I hate it when you're maternal. I'm older than you, remember?"

Caren smiled. "No matter how old we ever get, I'll never be as old as you. Someday I'm going to take a lot of pleasure in reminding you of that."

Laughing, Sarah got up and trotted down the steps, back to her bike. "Well, I guess I'd better get back home."

"So you can work, or dig up more skeletons?"

Sarah winked. "A little of both, probably. See you later."

She rode off, leaving them behind, and told herself that tomorrow she'd have some answers. If Caren was right, and Marcus Stephens had never lived in her house, then perhaps she could get over this preoccupation she had with him.

But if he had...

If he had, she would have to get to the bottom of these mysteries somehow. She didn't think she would have any choice.

CHAPTER THREE

The records were there for anyone to see. Sarah stared down at Marcus Stephens's name as one of the previous owners of her house, and she felt her heart trip into double time. From 1947 until the year she was born, he had lived in the same house she lived in, slept in the same room, eaten in the same kitchen....

What did it all mean?

She stumbled out of the office without thanking the clerk who had spent twenty minutes finding the records, and made her way to her car. She didn't get in, but instead stood at the door, staring at her own reflection in the window and trying to sort out what she had learned about Marcus Stephens.

He had loved a woman who looked like her, but had he known that she lived in this house? Had that, perhaps, confused him into thinking she *was* the woman in the picture?

Too many coincidences, she thought as she unlocked her door and forced herself to get in. No explanations. Just a man who had died for no good reason, and a volatile history that entangled their lives more with each passing day.

The car phone rang, startling her out of her reveries, and she reached for it, punched the send button and brought the headset to her ear. "Hello."

"Sarah, it's Mick. Are we still on for Friday night?"

Sarah frowned. Had she made plans with Mick, the creative director at the ad agency that gave her the most work, and forgotten? "Refresh my memory," she said vaguely.

"Sarah, the dinner party. It was your idea, for God's sake."

Clutching the phone between shoulder and ear, she tried to change lanes to get onto the interstate. He was right, she thought. It had been her idea to invite the execs of Sweeter-Than-Sin Yogurt over so that they could pick each other's brains about what look they wanted in her shoot without feeling as if they were in a board meeting. "Of course it was," she said, rallying. "And we're still on."

"And you're damn glad I reminded you, right?"

She smiled. "Right. I've been a little distracted the last few days."

"So I've heard. Pretty tough, what happened at the shoot the other day. You never know what kind of crazies are hanging around."

Her smile collapsed. "He wasn't a 'crazy.' He didn't do anything wrong."

"Right. And neither did John Hinkley until he pulled the trigger. Count your blessings, Sarah."

Sarah didn't answer. Some defensive reaction she couldn't explain, couldn't isolate, tightened her chest.

"Hey, are you okay?"

"Yeah, fine. Look, I'm just about to the temple. I'd better go."

"Temple?" he asked on a laugh. "Since when did you turn Jewish?"

"Not the Jewish temple, the Greek one. And I didn't convert. We're using it in the Elizabeth Arden ad, remember? Classic beauty, that sort of thing?"

"Oh, yeah. But that shoot isn't scheduled for two weeks, is it?"

"Preliminary work, pal. You do your job, and I'll do mine."

"Ouch. Okay, Sarah. Get back to me and I'll help with the party."

"Darn right you will. You're doing the cooking."

"I grill a mean steak, Sarah. Your house is gonna be great for this."

She pressed the end button and set the cellular phone back on its hook, thinking over the details she'd have to attend to for the party. She hoped it wouldn't rain that night. The whole idea of the thing was to cook out, relax and brainstorm. Being thrown together in a house with a leaky roof would be close to disastrous. She dreaded the thought already.

But it wasn't because of the rain, she thought. She dreaded it because she needed some time, time to herself, quiet time to spend with the box that held Marcus's life, in the house he had owned, thinking about how it all fit together....

Caren was right, she thought as she cut off her car in the parking lot of the Greek Orthodox temple. She was obsessing. But it was a puzzle that had to be solved, and Sarah rarely walked away from unanswered questions.

Obsessive or not, she was going to stay with this until it played itself out. The fact was, she had very little choice in the matter.

Sarah had forgotten about the film she'd ordered for the old camera until it arrived two hours before her party Friday night. Despite all she had to do before her guests arrived, she took a moment to load the camera, then put it aside for when she had time to play with it.

The steaks had all been marinated, the caterer had brought all the other food, and the sun was shining with bright promise of a dry night, even though the weatherman predicted a thirty-percent chance of showers that evening. Despite how crazy her week had been, with two more shoots, back-to-back creative meetings Wednesday and today and marathon sessions in her darkroom trying to achieve proofs of just the right shots to fulfill her clients' hopes and dreams, she had managed to pull tonight together.

It was funny, though, how much Marcus Stephens had been on her mind, even with everything else going on. And it was even funnier how she had managed to work in more hours of digging through his box, studying his pictures again and again, trying to fill in the years, the voids in his eyes, the holes in his past.

Yes, Caren was right. *Obsessive* was just the word for how she felt, and yet not even knowing that could make her stop. There was a void within her that was big enough to drive a Lincoln through, she told herself, and something about her connection with Marcus Stephens filled it.

But when the guests began to arrive, laughing and drinking and exuding excitement about the shoot she was doing for their ad, she felt herself being momentarily distracted from her ghostly thoughts of the man who had died. This was real life, she told herself, trying to join in their banter and their brainstorming. This was her life.

They had just finished eating when it began to drizzle, and as everyone filed into the house, Sarah grabbed the camera she'd found in the attic and shouted, "Smile, everybody."

Just as the camera snapped and the bulb flashed, a tiny jolt startled her, and she looked down at the camera, frowning. Had it been her imagination, or had it shocked her?

"Take another one, Sarah."

Sarah looked up at the crowd as they moved in closer for the picture. "All right, but think old. It'll be black-and-white, and this camera's so ancient it probably won't work anyway. But if it does, it might have a neat effect." She brought the viewfinder back to her eye, focused and snapped again.

Again she felt the jolt, and she looked down at the camera. Maybe it had come from the flash, she thought. Her curiosity piqued, she began to move her subjects around, experimenting more with the film. Still, with each flash, she felt the tiny shock.

"Will you give us copies for our bulletin board at work?" someone asked, shaking her out of her reverie. "That is, if they're not museum material?"

"I can promise you they won't be museum material," Sarah said with a laugh. "And if they come out at all, they're yours."

By the time the guests left, she had filled up the entire roll of film. Mick was the last to leave, and she found herself wishing he'd go so she could lock herself in the darkroom and see what she'd gotten.

But it was one of those nights, and Mick had something on his mind. "So, Sarah... When are you gonna let me tap some of that passion I see in your eyes?"

Sarah grinned at the man who'd been her friend for the past two years. If not for him, her career would never have reached the heights it had. She owed him big-time—but she didn't owe him her body. And as handsome and worldly as he was, she'd never had the slightest urge to be more than friends with him. He had plenty of women who did.

"Oh, I don't know," she said, gathering up the glasses littering the living room. "It would be a shame to ruin a perfectly good friendship."

"Might just take it to a new level," he said. "So what does a guy have to do? Wine and dine you? Send you roses?"

She smiled. "It would make a lot better impression than sprawling in my recliner and asking me to take off my clothes."

"I never did that."

"You might as well have."

He grinned and dropped the footrest, then sat up straight in the chair. "So...you're saying if I take you out to a nice, romantic dinner, say sweet things to you and give you flowers, I might get into your pants afterward?"

Sarah shook her head and faced him with an incredulous smile. "No doubt, Mick. In fact, just the thought of all that romance makes me want to jump you right now."

"I knew it. So let's go."

Sarah laughed. "You're incorrigible. It sounds intriguing, Mick, but I have some film to develop."

"You're going to regret this, you know."

"I know," Sarah said, taking the dishes into the kitchen. "My loss, I guess. I don't know how I'll sleep tonight."

"You're a cold woman, Sarah Rhinehart."

"I know," she said. "If only you could feel the chill."

"I do, and I'm going. Have fun in the darkroom, and meanwhile I'll just keep dreaming about getting you into another dark room." He pressed a kiss to her forehead and started out. "Hey, thanks for a great party. It really went over well."

Sarah locked the door behind him and turned back to face the mess that had been left behind. There was a lot to do, but somehow she couldn't make herself face it tonight.

Slowly, she walked back into the big living room, which, just half an hour ago, had been teeming with people. Now it was empty, but that was just the way she liked it, wasn't it? No demands, no pretense.

So why did the loneliness get bigger and quieter every night? Why did it fill up the house like a poison in the air, seeping into her lungs and making her want so badly to reach out to someone?

But not just anyone. Not Mick, and not any of the other men who'd made suggestive comments at her party. The truth was, hardly anyone would do.

She picked up the phone and dialed her sister. It rang three times before Jimmy answered.

"Hello?"

"Hey, Jimmy," she said. "Is Caren busy?"

"Uh..." She could hear the rustle of sheets, the squeak of a mattress. "No, just a minute."

She closed her eyes and sank to her chair as Caren came to the phone. "Hey, sis."

"I interrupted something. I'm sorry, Caren. I'll call tomorrow."

"Well, you might have interrupted a little something," she said, and then she heard whispered laughter. "Excuse me. I meant a *big* something." More laughter, and Sarah couldn't help smiling.

"Call me tomorrow, okay?"

"Is everything all right? Is the party over?"

"Yeah," Sarah said. "Everything's great. Get back to your husband."

She hung up the phone and let the smile linger on her face a few more moments as she stared at it. Caren was happy, and Sarah was truly happy for her. But somehow, deep in that little-girl part of her that still clung to her sister, she couldn't help feeling that she had lost something. Not her sister, exactly, but perhaps the exclusivity they'd shared, as each other's one and only best friend, before Caren had met Jimmy.

But that was the way it was supposed to be, wasn't it? People grew up, left their families and started families of their own. So why hadn't it happened for her?

Shaking off the depression sweeping over her, she got the camera and went into the darkroom, turned on the red light over her table and began to develop the film.

Her mind got lost in the routine of it, making her feel better, as being busy always did. She laughed aloud as some of the pictures began to develop. The quality left something to be desired, telling her instantly that she wouldn't be able to use this camera in her work, except in exceptional circumstances, but the shots she'd gotten of her guests were priceless.

She watched the last one as the faces blurred against the white paper and smiled at some of the silly expressions she'd caught as the whole crowd had looked her way. She saw Steven, the man who made the decisions about the ad agencies his company used, lighting a cigarette and hiking his eyebrow, and his wife, Beth, with her mouth wide open. Jerry Jackson, the marketing director, was bending over as if to moon her—something she would have loved to get on film just for its sheer blackmail value—and his partner, Trip Miller, rooting for him to do it. And then there was Mick, checking out Ellen's legs as she bent over the coffee table.

Her eyes scanned all of the faces as the pictures became crisp, and she reached for her magnifying glass to get a better look. She must have gotten everyone in that picture, she thought with a note of pride. No one had been left out, yet it was still a spontaneous, unposed shot. The Sweeter-Than-Sin people would love having this on their bulletin board. Maybe she'd make a print for each of them, sort of like a party favor. The goodwill gesture couldn't hurt business.

She started to hang up the print when something caught her eye, startling her. There was someone she hadn't seen in the picture, standing back in the shadows of her living room, staring into space with deep, brooding eyes....

Marcus Stephens.

She caught her breath, jerked the print off the line and held it under the light again. The magnifying glass enlarged his features, the dark, unkempt hair, the soft shadows beneath his eyes, the lips, pouted and set without purpose. It was the face she'd seen in the old pictures, the ones from when he was younger, after the war, when the spirit that could be seen in his eyes was ailing.

But he *couldn't* have been here.

She grabbed the other pictures, searched the faces for one that could be mistaken for Marcus's, someone she might have missed, a stranger, perhaps, or a friend whose resemblance to him she had never noticed.

But no one there looked anything like him.

She sank onto her stool and stared again, horrified, at his face.

How could someone who looked so much like him have been standing there, among her guests, without her seeing him?

Dropping the print, she bolted across the room to the box that held his things. With trembling hands, she dug for the pictures. The first one she grabbed was the one with him and the woman—the woman who looked just like her, but wasn't. Heart fluttering, she went back to the print she had taken tonight, with the man who looked just like him, but couldn't be.

There was no doubt, she thought with a wave of dizziness. It was him. It was crazy. And it was impossible.

But there he was. And there she was. And, somehow, she had to get to the bottom of this.

Obsessive, Caren had said, but she didn't know the half of it. And Sarah didn't think she could tell her. This was private, she thought, something between Marcus and her. Something that no one else could understand.

Marcus Stephens's appearance in her life had started some cataclysmic cycle that she knew she might never understand. But that didn't mean she would ever stop trying.

CHAPTER FOUR

Sleep was as elusive that night as understanding, and Sarah lay awake, looking around her at the shadows in her room, waiting for Marcus's face to materialize in some ghostly form. Was her house haunted? she asked herself. Was his ghost trying to speak to her, in the form of that picture and the box of his things?

Feeling a chill, she got up to find a blanket and found herself wandering through the big house, looking in every room, lingering in the shadows, trying to imagine him here in the same room, in the same house, looking at her with those brooding eyes.

When his image couldn't be conjured up by sheer force of will, she went back to the box and looked, once again, at the picture of Marcus with the woman.

Her heartbeat raced, as though it knew something she did not, and again she found herself sorting through his belongings, her fingertips lingering on each item, as if somewhere in the clutter lay the answers to all her questions.

Her hand fell on a book called *Lumen,* by Camille Flammarian, and she drew it out, flipped open the cover. Her eyes scanned the pages until she found a passage Marcus had underlined. It was about the relativity of time versus the absolutes perceived by the human mind. Frowning, she turned the page and scanned until she realized the story was about a man who had traveled through time.

Time travel, she thought with a chill that journeyed all the way up her spine. Time travel.

She pulled out the book on Einstein and opened it, turning the pages until she found another passage Marcus had marked, this one about the "narrow slit in a broad curtain" through which things are perceived. And in the margin Marcus had written, "Her time to my time; light waves through hole in curtain."

Her hands began to tremble, and she tried to absorb what he had said. *Her time . . .* Whose time?

She turned the pages faster, searching for more notes, and finally she came to a page where he had underlined a passage about the idea of time travel. At the top of the page, Marcus had written the word *Camera.*

The camera, she thought, her heart pounding out of control. She closed the book and stared at the picture of him with the woman, considering for the first time the possibility that it might, indeed, be her.

It couldn't be, she told herself, and yet it couldn't have been his face in the picture she had taken, either.

She grabbed the print still lying on the table, found his face in the shadows again and admitted finally that the key lay in that camera.

Light waves . . . hole in curtain . . . her time to my time . . .

What if . . . what if the camera enabled her to see through the hole in that curtain Einstein spoke of, from her time to Marcus's? If the curtain had opened long enough for her to see his face in her picture, what if she tried again?

Frantically, feverishly, she set up her tripod, reloaded the old camera and prepared it to take her own picture. There was a timer on it, probably one of the earliest ever made, and she set it and positioned herself on her stool.

As she waited for the camera to snap, she asked herself what she hoped to achieve. Another glimpse of him, maybe closer this time? A chance for him to glimpse her? Or perhaps for them to—for a split second—see each other at the same time?

It was madness, she told herself, and she was insane even to entertain the thought. She had almost convinced herself to stop the timer, put the camera away and go on back to bed when she heard the subtle click of the shutter. The bulb flashed.

She felt that jolt again, only this time it was stronger, fiercer, knocking her down. She hit the floor with an impact she hadn't expected, and a black dizziness washed over her. She felt suddenly ill, too ill to open her eyes, too sick to pick herself up, too weak to move.

For a moment she lay still, trying to catch her breath, and as she slowly managed to force her eyes open, she concentrated on the symmetry of the boards on the floor, the linear grooves, the predictable pattern. If she could just get to her knees, lift up her head...

A cuckoo sounded, startling her, and as though the fright shot her with enough adrenaline to lift her head, she looked up and saw the clock that Stella had kept, Marcus Stephens's clock. Only...how had it gotten into her darkroom?

A sheen of perspiration glistened over her face as it slowly occurred to her that it wasn't her darkroom, because the furnishings were different. Yet it was the same window, the same molding along the ceiling, the same placement of the door....

"Who are you?"

She swung around at the deep, surprised voice, and wobbled as the face of the man standing in the doorway came into focus. "Oh, my God!"

"I asked you who you are," he repeated. "How did you get into my house?"

His face grew closer—the face of the young Marcus Stephens, just like that in the pictures in the box— and the room began to spin. Her stomach tried to revolt, but weakness washed over her. She opened her mouth, making an effort to speak, to explain what even she could not understand, but her throat closed up. The room began to fade into blackness, but still the spinning went on.

She dropped back to the floor, felt the cold planks beneath her burning face, and as the horror of possibility rose up inside her, her world went black and she lost herself in the spinning infinity of a reality she couldn't explain.

And the questions didn't matter anymore.

Sarah woke to a brightness, and comfort sweet and soft couched her weak, tired body. Someone was wiping her forehead with a cold, wet rag, gently, sweetly....

He bent over her, his face racked with concern. The face she had obsessed over, fantasized over, studied over. Eyes that had looked at her from an old man's face now beheld her from a young man's.

"You..." she whispered, but he touched her mouth with his fingertips.

"Shh. You're too weak to talk."

His voice was scratchy-deep, cultured, honey-smooth. "You're...Marcus..."

"Marcus Stephens," he said, and she realized he was looking not into her eyes, but *at* them. "Can you tell me your name?"

"Sarah," she whispered, and waited for a hint of recognition from him. There was none.

She felt the nausea rising like the fear that shivered through her, but she fought it back. "What...what year is this?"

He smiled. "You *are* confused, aren't you?"

She shook her head, impatient for an answer. "Tell me."

"Nineteen fifty-three," he said, his smile fading. "Do you have any other lapses in your memory?"

Tears sprang to her eyes, and she tried to put together the words to explain—that there weren't lapses in memory at all, just a curtain separating time, and a camera, and two people who knew each other who couldn't have.

The nausea rose higher, and she tried to sit up.

"No," he ordered. "Lie still."

"Sick," she managed to say, then covered her mouth with her palm.

Quickly he handed her a bowl and watched with a doctor's calm as she retched into it until there was nothing left. Finally she dropped her head back to the pillow and closed her eyes. "It did something to me," she whispered. "The travel."

"How far did you come?" he asked.

"Decades," she whispered.

She heard some movement, but couldn't open her eyes to look. He left the room and came back moments later, and suddenly she felt an avalanche of ice falling on and around her, and she began to fight.

"Lie still," he ordered, getting onto the bed with her to hold her still. "You're burning with fever, and you're dehydrated. Lie still, damn it. I'm going to call an ambulance."

"No!" The shouted word had more energy packed into it than she possessed, but she couldn't take the chance of his not heeding her protest. "No hospital. Please!"

She began to shiver uncontrollably, and he released his hold on her and packed the ice around her neck and arms and, taking a handful, held it to her face. "Please! You don't understand!"

"*You* don't understand," he said. "You could die."

"I thought you were a doctor," she cried.

"I'm not even practicing anymore," he said. "I'm not equipped for this. You need tests, drugs. I can't help you here."

"I'm all right," she whimpered. "Please, don't take me out of this house. I don't know what might happen."

"Are you in trouble?" he asked. "With the law or..."

She shook her head, and tears filled her eyes. "No, not that. It's molecular laws. Physical laws." Helpless to make sense of it, she let the tears spill down her temples and seep into her hair. "Oh, God, you could never understand. Just...promise me you won't take me out of this house."

Her sobs grew in substance and strength, and suddenly she realized he had lain down next to her and was putting his arms around her, ignoring the ice and the cold. Still shivering, she curled into him, weeping against his shirt for all the confusion and misery and illness she felt at that very moment, but even more for all that she knew was to come.

For she knew now, as she had never realized before, that her coming here had completed some cycle she was destined to complete. But it had to change this time, or it would stay in that neat, tragic circle for eternity, forever turning, repeating, living, dying.

There was something here that she couldn't fathom. But all she knew for certain was that she'd never felt a sense of peace or belonging greater than she felt right here, in Marcus Stephens's arms.

She was so small, Marcus thought as her tears bled the strength out of her, and he held her closer, wondering why it felt so right. All he knew of her was that her name was Sarah, that she'd been hallucinating, that she was very ill. Nothing else she'd said made any sense.

He felt her relax as sleep began to claim her, and the thought occurred to him again that he should get her to a hospital. But she'd been so adamant....

He looked down at her as her eyes closed and her breathing returned to normal. The ice around her had melted, and the bed sheets were wet. Her hair was soaked and tangled from her struggle with whatever this illness was, and he was wet, too, from holding her.

Her fever had begun to break, he thought as he felt the mist of perspiration on her brow. She needed dry clothes and linens.

Slowly slipping his arms out from under her, he got up and looked down at her. She looked almost like a child, lying curled on his bed, and yet she was far from a child. Her breasts strained against her wet gown, full and promising, reminding him of desires he had long ago buried. Reminding him that he was still a man.

Gently he sat on the edge of the bed and opened the top button of her gown. She didn't stir. Slowly he released the buttons all the way down, until the swell of her breasts was visible, until his own body reacted shamelessly.

You're a doctor, he reminded himself. He had to look at her with a clinical eye. She had come to him for help, had somehow found him despite the locked doors, and that made her his patient. He had no right to lust for a patient, no matter how long it had been since he'd been alone with a woman.

Pushing back the desire accelerating his own pulse, he peeled her wet gown off her shoulders and tried not to notice how her nipples grew turgid, the heaviness of her breasts, the tiny curve of her waist.

He swallowed, but his mouth had gone dry.

He went to his bureau, opened a drawer and pulled out a folded T-shirt. It would swallow her, he thought with amusement, but he didn't want her to get chilled, so he slid it over her head, his movements deft and economical, professional and precise.

He lifted her in his arms then, felt how light and weak she was, and quietly he laid her on the sofa against his window. Then, quickly, he stripped the wet bedclothes, dried the plastic covering the mattress and remade the bed.

She never stirred as he lifted her again and laid her back on the bed, then pulled up the blankets and covered her.

He pulled a chair to the side of the bed and sat down, watching her. She was beautiful, he thought. Even with her hair tangled from sickness, even with the dark circles beneath her eyes, even with her skin as pale as paper.

He wondered how her eyes changed when she smiled, and he hoped he would find out when she woke tomorrow. He needed a smile in his life, he thought. Maybe, for a moment, that would chase away some of the ghosts.

He touched her wrist, timed her pulse and realized that she was stabilizing. She would be all right, he thought, as long as she didn't take a turn for the worse. He would sit by her all night, if necessary, until he was certain she was out of danger.

* * *

Dawn painted the room a brighter color when Sarah opened her eyes again. It was her room, she thought with a breath of relief, and the breeze whispering through the curtains cooled her skin, which finally felt normal again.

It had been a dream, she thought. She hadn't traveled through time to find the man who'd been intruding upon her every thought. She had been lying here in her own bed all this time, and now the sunlight, warm and bright and healthy, was putting everything back into perspective.

"How do you feel?"

She jerked her head around at the voice and saw Marcus Stephens sitting beside the bed, clearly worn from keeping vigil beside her. Slowly she sat up. "It wasn't a dream."

He reached out for her forehead, frowned at the feel of it, then moved to sit on the bed and take her wrist in his hand. "Your fever's gone. And your pulse is back to normal."

She raked her fingers through her hair and stared at him, as if seeing him for the first time. "I—I feel fine. Like I was never sick."

"How could that be?" he asked. "You must feel weak or something."

She shook her head. "No. I feel refreshed, like I've had a good night's sleep."

She looked down at the man's T-shirt she wore and quickly covered her breasts. "You...you changed my clothes."

"I had to," he said. "You were soaking wet from the ice."

"Oh." She met his eyes, suddenly self-conscious at the way she looked, at what he might have seen when he'd undressed her, at what he thought of her after seeing her vomit, shiver, cry. . . .

"So. . . are you ready to tell me what's going on?"

"Going on?" she asked.

"Yes. The reason you were so adamant about not going to the hospital. The reason you would break into my house rather than make your way there in the first place."

"I didn't break into your house," she said. "It's my house. Or. . . it was. . . ."

"You lived here before?"

She seemed flustered by the question, and she shook her head. "This is all crazy," she said. "How I got here in the first place . . . the sickness. . . ."

"Has this ever happened to you before? A violent illness that disappeared in a matter of hours?"

"Never," she said. "But I've never traveled like this before." A darkness fell over her face, and she frowned, as if trying to piece something together. "I guess it makes sense, though. You couldn't travel at such speeds without having some sort of molecular change in your body."

"What speed? Where did you come from?"

She drew in a heavy breath and shook her head. "Could I take a shower or something, get dressed, maybe eat . . . before we get into this?"

He smiled. "Of course. But you do realize, don't you, that you showed up here in your gown? I washed it out last night, but it isn't dry yet. I could give you something of mine."

She shrugged. "Whatever."

He got up and pulled a big shirt out of his drawer, handed it to her. "It's big enough to cover you, until your gown dries. The bathroom's in there. I'll make you breakfast while you shower. Are you sure you're strong enough?"

"Yes," she said.

"Okay." He went to the door of his bedroom, offering her privacy, then turned back. Sitting up like this, her hair mussed and her breasts pushing beneath the jersey of his T-shirt, she looked even more sexual than Marilyn Monroe. He turned his face away. "Call if you need anything."

She nodded quietly, and he closed the door behind him.

Leaning against the door, he told himself not to get his hopes up. He knew nothing about her, except that she made him feel alive again. And somehow, he didn't trust that feeling.

And he certainly couldn't expect her to hang around here much longer. She had come to him sick, and now she was well.

But he could enjoy her company for as long as he had it. And maybe, he thought with a tiny thrill of apprehension, just maybe, it would be the start of something good in his life.

Sarah stood beneath the spray of the shower, letting it wash away the residue of her illness. But it couldn't wash away the fear.

She rinsed the soap from her hair, let the lather ribbon down over her shoulders, her stomach, down her legs to the floor. She was standing here, in this shower that was identical to her shower, just as she would on any other day, in her own home—only it wasn't hers. It was his.

The camera had sent her back, through that curtain in time. But what if the curtain didn't open again? The camera was still in her time, after all. It wasn't as if she could ask someone for help or have someone send her back.

What if she was stuck here, and she never had the chance to go back and tell her sister what had happened? What if she never saw Caren again, and she was forever lost in this time with this man?

Tears came to her eyes, and she squeezed them shut and let the shower spray down over them. How could she explain this to Marcus? Would he judge her insane and send her away? And if he did, where would she go?

She cried until the water turned cold, then forced herself to pull herself together, get out and dry herself. She looked around for a blow dryer, then remembered there would be no such thing. They hadn't been invented yet.

She combed out her hair, then left it wet and pulled on his big shirt, which hung to her knees. Despite the way it covered her, she still felt naked.

Weary from crying, she stepped out of the bathroom.

"Are you all right?" He was waiting for her, and his eyes swept the length of her, from her wet hair to her slender legs to her bare feet.

"Yes," she said. "I'm fine."

"I was worried you might have fainted or something."

"No," she said. "I told you, I don't even feel weak. I'm well, I think." She smiled. "You must be a good doctor."

"I'm not a doctor...not anymore," he said. "At least, not a practicing one. Haven't you heard?"

"Yeah," she whispered. "I guess I had heard that. Why is that?"

He shrugged off her question and started out of the room. "There's breakfast made," he said. "You need to eat. But not too much. Your stomach will be a little shaky after last night."

She followed him on the hardwood floor, the same floor she had walked on hundreds of times, only in her time it was older, duller. Now it looked clean and shiny, fresh, younger. She'd have to have it redone when she got back, she thought. Maybe she could get it back to the original shine.

When she got back...

Again tears sprang to her eyes, and she sat down at the plate he'd set for her. She wasn't aware he was watching her until he ordered, "Eat."

Obeying, she picked up a piece of buttered toast. "It's good," she said quietly. "Thank you."

He didn't touch the food he had before himself, but stared at her instead. "How did you hear about me?"

She shook her head. "You wouldn't believe me if I told you."

"Try me. I haven't practiced around here in over two years. Why would anyone have sent you to me when there's a hospital less than a mile away?"

"I wasn't sent, exactly," she said, meeting his eyes.

"Then why did you come?" His gaze was intense, piercing, confused. "And how did you get in here? All the doors were locked."

Those tears billowed in her eyes, and she shook her head again. "I don't know."

He took her hand, forced her eyes back to his. "Yes, you do. Tell me. Who are you, and how did you get here?"

"I'm Sarah Rhinehart." Those tears wouldn't let go of her, and she leaned forward, trying to find the words to make him understand. "It's crazy, and it doesn't make any sense. But it happened nonetheless."

"What happened?"

She drew in a deep breath and decided there was no way to say it without simply saying it. "Do you believe in time travel?"

He dropped her hand and stared at her, his expression unchanged. "What?"

"Marcus, I'm not from here... from now. I found the camera, and you were in the picture, and there was a jolt, and I didn't know what might happen, but..."

Her voice trailed off when she saw the look on his face, a look that reflected what he was probably thinking. *Tread lightly, she's still not right.* He must think she was crazy.

"You're still confused, aren't you?" he asked quietly.

She nodded, though she knew she wasn't.

"Can you stay a while for observation? I'd like to watch you a while before you go back."

"I don't know if I *can* go back," she whispered, and those tears stole into her eyes again.

"Why not?" he asked. "What kind of trouble are you in?"

She drew in a deep sigh that seemed to reach clear to her soul. "I don't know, Marcus. I really don't know."

He took her hand and squeezed it, and the touch sent rays of warmth into her heart, which had been desolate for so long. "You can stay here as long as you need to," he said. "And when you feel ready to talk, I'll listen."

The warmth of his words, his understanding about secrets that were too convoluted to be explained, filtered through her like warm honey, but the sheer sweetness of it made the tears come more freely.

She tried to eat, but it was hard to swallow, not because she'd been ill, but because it was too much, sitting here with this man who had filled her thoughts every waking moment. She glanced up at him through her misty eyes, watched him bring the toast to his lips, bite a piece, chew. His eyes were the pastel color of a springtime sky, but there was a pall over them, a sadness, much like the sadness she had seen in him as an old man. His hair was tousled and badly in need of a cut, and the circles under his eyes shadowed into his face, just as she had seen them in the picture of him among her party guests. He needed a shave, and she wondered how that stubble would feel on his jaw, against her hand, against her lips. He had a nice jaw, she thought, a strong jaw, and his face held great character and even greater compassion. Beyond that, she could see the integrity there, the unwavering rightness within him... a rightness that brooked no grays in a black-and-white world. A rightness that could never tolerate how she had gotten here to him.

His shirt was open halfway down, and he reached up to his chest, scratched the tip of his thumb through the hair covering it. His chest hair curled thickly up to his neck, and she wondered how it would feel against her fingers. Would it be soft? Would it have a taste all its own?

He smiled slightly; somehow it seemed foreign to him. "Your hair's getting your shirt wet."

She glanced down and realized that her hair had wet the front of the shirt, molding it to her breasts, and she crossed her arms to cover them. She felt her face warming, and she knew it was turning pink. That was why Caren always told her that her every thought was written across her face, in living color.

"I need a blow dryer...."

"A what?"

"Never mind. What do women do...about wet hair, I mean?"

He frowned. "They sit under the hair dryer...don't they?"

She smiled. "You wouldn't have one, would you?"

His laughter was unexpected. "Sorry. I dropped out of beauty school to be a doctor."

She chuckled, herself. "And why did you drop out of medicine?"

His smile faded, and he looked down at the plate of food before him. "I didn't belong there."

She kept her eyes on him. "Why?"

"I just didn't." He pushed back his chair and took his plate to the kitchen.

Sarah sat still, and suddenly a chill swept over her. She had crossed over the bounds, pried into something he didn't want to talk about.

She got up, took her own plate and went into the kitchen, which looked remarkably like her own, except for the absence of the few updated appliances that had been installed since then. "I'm sorry," she said.

He scraped his plate into a wastebasket and set it in the sink. "For what?"

"For prying. It's none of my business."

"No problem." He took her plate, scraped what was left and set it in the sink, as well.

She stood back, watching, as he ran water into the sink, squirted some dishwashing soap into it and began to wash.

She stepped forward and stopped him. "Let me. You've done so much, and you're tired."

"I'll wash and you dry," he said.

Acquiescing, she got the towel and began to dry the breakfast dishes. She felt the heat emanating from him, the masculinity, the vibrant smell of man. Awareness sizzled in the room, charging the atmosphere with something she'd never felt, and she suddenly became blatantly aware of the nothing she wore under his shirt.

"I wonder if my gown is dry," she whispered.

He finished the last dish and dried his hands. "I doubt it. I rinsed it out, and it'll probably be hours before it's ready to wear again." He smiled and glanced at the shirt hanging loosely over her body. "You don't like wearing my shirt? It looks a hell of a lot better on you than it does on me."

She smiled. "It's fine."

For a moment they just looked at each other, and Sarah's heart began to pound in a rhythm no percussionist could have matched. She wondered if he knew the effect he had on her, how he made her mouth go dry, made her heart hammer, made the junction between her thighs ache....

She wondered how long it had been since he'd been with a woman. And she tried to remember the last time she'd been with a man.

His chest rose with the intake of breath. "I don't know who you are, Sarah Rhinehart," he whispered, "but, God, you're so beautiful."

Some final wall of fear melted inside her, turning her insides to hot, wet wax that flowed like blood through her veins. "I don't know how long I'll be here," she whispered. "It could be a long time ... or just a few more minutes. I don't know."

"Stay a while," he told her.

His face began to descend to hers, and she felt herself lifting, as if on wings, though her feet were still on the ground. "I want to know you, Marcus," she whispered. "I want to know everything about you."

His hand moved to touch her face, and suddenly his lips caught hers, soft and sensuous. Their lips fit perfectly together, and his tongue moved urgently into her mouth, dancing softly against hers, measuring, tasting, taunting, until she stood on her toes and slid her arms around his neck.

His hair was soft to the touch, and it feathered through her fingers. His head moved as her fingertips massaged across his scalp, and she felt his tiny intakes of breath as he lost himself in her touch. His hand slid down to the small of her back, and he pulled her more tightly against him.

She felt his tumescence through his pants, and while it sent a tingle sparking through her core, she reveled in the sweet power it gave her, as well. But it gave him a power, too, a power so strong that it ruled her head, even as he commanded her heart.

You can't sleep with him, some voice in her mind cried out. You don't even know him. She wasn't the kind of woman to take that kind of thing lightly. But what if her chance ended and she never saw him again?

The sheer unreality of the whole moment made it right—in much the same way that a dream was right—and when his hand slid beneath her shirt, stroked the soft curve of her hip, then lingered at the triangle of hair, she wanted to be rid of her shirt and his shirt, wanted to have her breasts pressed against his skin....

As if he read her mind, or the moisture he felt when he touched her, he lifted her quickly and carried her to his bed.

She wanted him to rip the shirt off her, tear his own clothes off and take her with the force and intensity with which this whole ordeal had assaulted her. Instead, he let her feet fall to the floor, looked down at her with smoky blue eyes that she knew had branded his signature on her heart and gazed at her as his breath grew heavier.

"I don't want to take advantage of you," he whispered.

"You won't be," she said.

"But just hours ago you were so sick, and you still don't—"

She touched her fingertips to his lips and whispered, "Shh... Now's the only moment that matters. I don't want to lose it."

His kiss was deep and fierce, and as he pulled his shirt over his head, she let her own drop to the floor.

A low, agonized moan escaped his throat as he beheld her, standing softly before him, and slowly he let his hand feather over her breast, her stomach, her hip....

"You're so beautiful," he whispered again.

"And so are you."

He lifted her again and laid her gently on the bed, and as he stepped out of his trousers and anchored her to the mattress, she abandoned herself to the completeness she had never found in her own time. The sense of absoluteness. The sense of oneness.

This was what Jimmy and Caren must have found. And she had traveled so far to find it, she hoped never to lose it again. Even if she had to sacrifice her whole world to hold on to it.

They made love with fierce abandon, then shared an almost violent climax, so painful in its pleasure that it threatened to bury them both in the avalanche of delirium that fell over them.

As soon as he could breathe again, Marcus raised up on one elbow and gazed down at her. "Please, Sarah.

I have to know where you came from. Can't you tell me?''

She touched his face, savoring the feel of his beard against her palm. "Will you promise to try to believe me, no matter how outrageous it sounds?"

"I promise," he whispered.

"All right." She took a deep breath and tried to find the right words. "A couple of weeks ago, I was working..."

Sarah! Sarah, where are you?

Her words trailed off. The voice seemed to come from far away, echoing in and out of her subconscious, distracting her from her explanation. She looked around and heard her sister's voice again.

Sarah! Are you here?

"Sarah..." It was Marcus's voice this time, and she jerked her head around, but even as she did, she felt herself leaving, pulling out of his time and reaching for her sister's voice, unable to stop herself.

"Marcus..."

She saw the horror on his face as his fingers slipped through her hand, as she faded from before him, as she wilted once again and felt the dizziness wash over her.

"Sarah!"

But it was too late, for her sister's voice wouldn't be hushed, and it alone was pulling her back.

Sarah closed her eyes and surrendered to the voice as the world went black around her.

CHAPTER FIVE

She was gone.

Marcus stared at the space where she had lain, naked and beautiful, just seconds ago, where he had touched her and watched her and listened to her. Her scent still lingered in the air, on his sheets, on his skin.

She hadn't been a figment of his imagination, he insisted to himself, and yet she was gone, like a ghost that had dissolved in midair.

How far did you come?

Decades.

The words sent a shiver through him, and he shook his head, unable to believe in such phenomena, unable to face what she had been trying to tell him when she faded out of his sight.

The thought that he'd finally snapped, locked up day after day, night after night, in this dismal, dark house, with nothing but his own recriminations to keep him comfort, nothing but the restless souls of dead men he hadn't saved, and that of the child whose face kept flashing through his mind . . .

He had seen it before, when he'd been practicing. Grief—the overwhelming kind that couldn't be faced alone—the kind that led to insanity or suicide . . . or both. He had snapped, and his mind was playing games with him. Games of beautiful women appearing in his house, needing him to save them, only to be snatched away at the moment of reconciliation.

That was it, he thought. She had never really been here. His mind had staged the whole thing, and as long as he could face that, see it clearly, perhaps he hadn't lost his faculties entirely. All he had to do was convince himself that she wasn't real and then he could set about trying to find his way back to himself.

Trembling, he got off the bed, rumpled from lovemaking so intense and memorable that he couldn't bear to think it had been a dream. But it must have been.

Still, the chair sat beside the bed, where he had kept vigil all night. And on the floor were the bedclothes that had been wet from last night. Still, that proved nothing, except that his response to his mind's games had been real.

There was nothing here to prove that she had ever entered his life, nothing more than an extra plate drying in the sink, a wet shower, a rumpled pillow.

And then he saw the gown.

It was hanging over a chair, still damp from the ice, long and sweet and . . . hers.

He knew he hadn't had that gown in the house before she'd come here, and as mad as he could admit to being, he couldn't explain where it had come from.

Unless she had really been here, flesh and blood, with that raging fever that had disappeared as quickly as she had.

Do you believe in time travel?

He grabbed the gown, brought it to his face and tried to imagine the warmth of her body in it.

Slowly he fell to his knees, and for the first time since he could remember he prayed to a God he had almost forgotten, that he wasn't insane, that he hadn't imagined her, and that, please God, she would come back to him.

If there was a thing called time travel, if she had indeed found him once, couldn't she find him again?

And if not, what would it take for him to find her?

Years, some voice in the back of his mind answered. It would take years.

Decades.

Somehow, he decided, he would find Sarah Rhinehart again.

Even if it took the rest of his life.

The world was spinning, and something threatened to revolt in Sarah's stomach as she strained to open her eyes to the chaos whirling around her.

Something was clamped to her face, and there were people hovering over her, lifting her, pricking things into her arm, jerking her.

"Oh, Sarah..."

She heard her sister's voice again, and, turning her head, she tried to focus on the blurry image of Caren. She was crying and reaching out for her. But someone was taking her away.

"Caren..." she whispered, surprised at the weakness in her own voice.

"I'm here, Sarah. They're taking you to the hospital. You're going to be fine."

But Caren didn't look as if she believed a word of it. Sarah closed her eyes as the spinning grew worse, as her stomach roiled and churned, as her head ached and her muscles throbbed. Vaguely she wondered what damage she had done to herself and whether she would recover as easily this time.

She felt herself being loaded into an ambulance, heard strange voices talking all around her, saw Caren getting in beside her. She looked up at her sister and thought of explaining to calm her down. *It was just the time travel, sis. Don't worry. I'll probably be over this in a few hours.*

But that would frighten Caren even more, and the next time she woke up she'd be in a straitjacket in a padded cell. Crazy. It was all too crazy to confide. No one would ever believe it.

She could hardly believe it herself.

She closed her eyes as the ambulance began to move, and the sweet oblivion of fevered nothingness made it all seem tolerable for a while.

Caren was still with her when Sarah woke in a hospital bed, with an IV in her arm and an oxygen tube in her nose. She felt the nausea taking hold of her, and quickly she sat up, reached for a bedpan and retched into it.

Caren waited patiently, holding the pan, until Sarah dropped back onto the pillows. "Are you feeling *any* better, Sarah?"

"Better than what?" Sarah asked.

"Better than you were when I found you." When Sarah only closed her eyes and failed to answer, Caren touched her forehead. "Oh, Sarah, I was so scared. I came in and called you, and then I heard this loud thump on the floor in your bedroom. Did you fall out of bed, or pass out, or what?"

"I don't know," she said.

"You were completely naked," Caren said, "and burning up with fever, and convulsing. Oh, it was the worst thing I've ever seen in my life. If I hadn't found you, there's no telling what might have happened to you."

Sarah tried hard to find some way to grasp the reality of what seemed so unreal. Had her sister's voice been the force that called her back? Had it been that simple? And what if she'd had more time with Marcus? Just a little more time to bask in his affection, his appreciation, his admiration. He had treated her like a breath of fresh air, a drastic relief for a troubled heart. He needed her, just as she needed him. It was all so perverse, her needing a man she had met before she'd even been born. It was all so tragic.

And yet she knew that as soon as she could she would go back to him.

"I want to go home," she whispered.

Caren shook her head. "You're too sick. They're doing tests on you, Sarah. They're going to find what's wrong with you."

"They won't find anything," she whispered. "And anyway, in a few hours I'll be well."

"How can you say that? Sarah, you don't realize how sick you are."

"Trust me," Sarah said. "I'll walk out of here like nothing ever happened. I just have to get through this for a few more hours."

"I won't let you," Caren said. "Now don't start pulling that stubborn act on me. If I didn't love you, I wouldn't care."

"Love is such a relative thing," she said weakly, as her eyes drifted shut again. "So much like time."

Just as she'd predicted, Sarah's illness disappeared as quickly as it had come. She got up and dressed in the clothes Jimmy had gotten from her house and insisted on sleeping in her own bed that night. Unable to come up with any other diagnosis, the doctors wrote her illness off as a virus, which they declared had been fully cured.

It took some doing to convince her sister that she truly was okay and force her to go home to her husband and let Sarah spend the night in her own home alone, but finally Caren acquiesced.

That night, when she was finally alone, Sarah wandered through the rooms of her house, trying to come to terms with what had happened to her. She had met Marcus Stephens, had made love to him, had fallen in love with him.

Somehow, she had to risk going back to him, despite the violent way her health had been affected by the experience.

But that night, as she lay on the bed in the room in which she'd made love to Marcus Stephens, she began to cry for what they had begun to share, for what had been cut off too soon.

And as sleep stalked her, she told herself that somehow they would finish what they'd started.

For she couldn't bear the thought of his growing old to find her, only to die before they had even exchanged a smile.

The doorbell rang, startling Marcus out of a light, fitful sleep, and the sudden hope blossomed in his heart that it was Sarah—that somehow the disappearance itself had been the aberration and not Sarah's entire existence. What if she stood on the other side of that door, waiting to fall into his arms as if they had known each other for an eternity, with or without explanation?

He flung the door open, but only Gene Fair confronted him. His heart collapsed like a diseased organ, and he stepped back from the door, disappointment etched in every line of his face.

"My God, man, you look like hell."

Marcus left the door and went to the couch in the middle of the room. Slumping on it, he covered his face. Gene closed the door behind him and joined Marcus on the couch. "What do you want, Gene?"

"I wanted to make sure you weren't dead and rotting in here."

"And what if I was?"

"Then I guess I'd dispose of what was left and put your house up for sale."

Marcus cracked a look at him, and Gene smiled.

"It's time you put yourself back together, you know. The hospital needs you."

"That's too bad. I told you, I'm through with medicine."

"How can you be?" Gene came off the couch and strolled across the floor, the heels of his loafers clicking on the wooden planks. "Mark, in med school it was you who kept me propped up. Remember that Christmas when I said I wasn't coming back? It wasn't worth it? And you practically dragged me back with your bare hands and forced me to finish?"

"You wanted to quit for a stupid reason. You had the hots for that Betty What's-Her-Name and couldn't stand to be away from her."

Gene paused and thought about the woman who had almost cost him his career. "Yeah, and she almost would have been worth it. Until she took up with that oboe player and got herself knocked up." He shrugged, as if it didn't matter anymore. "There was another time, too. Remember when we were residents, and I'd been on for forty hours—you had, too—and I was practically suicidal. 'Nothing is worth this,' I said, and you told me that someday we'd look back and laugh." He bent over Marcus, forced him to look up at him. "Why aren't you laughing, man?"

Marcus met his eyes without amusement. "Because there are things worse than being on a forty-hour shift, Gene."

"Look, I'm not trying to discount what you went through in Korea, man. But whatever it was, it can't be bad enough to turn your back on everything. How are you gonna make a living?"

Marcus raked his hands through his dirty hair and ran his fingers over his jaw, the same jaw Sarah had touched with such softness, such sweetness. "I don't know," he said quietly. "Research, maybe."

"Research? Man, you'd be wasting yourself. You're a surgeon. You can't just give that up!"

"Watch me."

"Damn it." Gene plopped back down on the couch and looked around him. "You got a beer or anything?"

"Nothing," Marcus said.

"Nothing? You look like you've been on a two-week drunk, and you're telling me you don't have any booze in the house?"

"That's what I'm telling you."

"So why do you look like you're riding the crest of a hangover? You look even worse than the last time I saw you."

Marcus's eyes glossed over, and he stared off into space. "I haven't been sleeping well," he said. "I've been having some dreams...."

"What kind of dreams? Sex dreams?"

Marcus offered Gene a tentative grin. "Maybe, Dr. Freud."

"Great," Gene said. "This I can relate to. Was there a woman involved?"

"Yeah." The word came out on a soft whisper, and his eyes focused on the nothingness again.

"Now we're getting somewhere. Was she a movie star? Audrey Hepburn? Elizabeth Taylor? I always have some wild dreams about that one, myself. You know, I met her once, when I was in LA. Damn, those eyes of hers.''

"Not a movie star," Marcus whispered. "A real woman. Flesh and blood.''

"As if Liz isn't. Okay, so is it someone you know?"

He thought for a moment, then whispered, "Yeah."

"So what's the holdup? Call the woman and take her out."

"I can't." He got up, went to the window. The drapes hadn't been opened in weeks, and no light had intruded on his cocoon at all. He thought of opening them now, but decided there was more comfort in darkness.

"You want me to do a little matchmaking for you? Tell me her name and I'll—"

"Just let it go, all right?" Marcus snapped. He caught the surprise on Gene's face and tried to soften his tone. "It's not like you think, okay? It was . . . just a dream."

"Sorry."

Marcus leaned back against the windowsill, and at once felt the desolation of his house without her in it. The loneliness was like a living thing, something that was smothering him, and yet it was something that held him like a drug held an addict. "I appreciate your coming by, man. I'm gonna be all right. I just need some time alone."

"That's all you've had since you got back from overseas, Mark. Don't you see that's exactly what you *don't* need? You've got to find something to make your life worth living again. But you're not going to find it cooped up in this house. It isn't just going to drop out of the sky, you know.''

Marcus's eyes glazed over again. ''You might just be surprised, Gene,'' he whispered. ''You never know what might fall out of the sky.''

CHAPTER SIX

A longing deeper than any Sarah had ever experienced took root in her soul for the next few days as she began to jog and exercise to get in shape for another visit with Marcus. It didn't matter that she would have to endure the violent sickness that went with it. All that mattered was seeing this through, finishing what had been started, what had come full circle when the old man had run in front of that car.

He was dead, and that thought sent a surge of grief through her. Dead before he'd even met her. Dead before she'd had the chance to change things.

Yet now she did have a chance.

She passed the abandoned church a mile from her house and pushed herself into the second mile. Tears welled up in her eyes, and she told herself that she simply couldn't allow that circle to continue on and on and on. His growing old to find the woman who had made such a volatile, intense appearance in his life. What must life have been like for him? Had he truly waited for her to be born, to grow up?

Unbidden, the image of a bouquet of balloons in the park came to her mind, and of Caren begging their aunt and uncle for one. Sarah had gotten hers first and, in her stubbornness, had refused to have it tied to her arm as Caren had. She had run through the park, watching the balloon bob over her head, laughing and shouting that it would take flight at any moment and transport her through the sky.

He had been there, she thought suddenly as she slowed to a stop on the bridge. He had been standing there, laughing and watching her, and it hadn't been until the balloon had slipped through her little fingers that she had even seen him.

She remembered screaming, as if something vital to her had been ripped away, but the man had heroically caught it, brought it back to her, squatted down in front of her and tied it to her wrist. "It won't get away again," he said.

It was Marcus, she thought, stopping cold and staring into the space of her memories as they played out before her. He hadn't waited until he was old to watch her. He had watched her all along.

She wiped the tears from her face and leaned against the rail on the bridge, looked over into the water and tried to pull herself together.

She heard a car behind her, and heard her sister's voice. "Sarah, are you all right?"

She turned around and smeared the tears away. "Hi, sis. Yeah, I'm fine."

"Were you coming to my house?"

"Yeah."

Caren put her car in park and opened the passenger door. "Get in, Sarah."

"No," she replied. "I was running. Trying to get into shape."

"You shouldn't be doing that," Caren argued. "You were in the hospital just yesterday. Now get in."

Deciding she could run again later, she got in, closed the door and closed her eyes against the cool air-conditioning blowing into her face.

"Sarah, this would probably be no big deal, except that you don't run. You hate running. Even when we were kids, you finagled a way out of it every time."

Sarah stared through the windshield. "I guess being sick just reminded me how badly I need exercise." She looked at her sister. "Caren, can I ask you something?"

"What?"

"Do you remember that time we were in the park and we had those balloons, and mine got away?"

Caren was quiet for a moment. "Not really. We had hundreds of balloons. And yours always got away because you were too stubborn to let Aunt Edith tie it to your wrist."

"Right," Sarah said. "But do you remember that time that man caught my balloon for me before it got too far, and he tied it to my wrist?"

"What man?"

"A man," Sarah said. "Don't you remember?"

"No," Caren said. "But I remember that time Uncle Will and I played that trick on you where he made you think the balloon had carried me off...."

"No, not that time," Sarah said impatiently. "I'm talking about something else."

"Well, sorry," Caren said. "I don't remember that."

Sarah dropped her head back on the seat of the car and was quiet until Caren's car pulled into her driveway.

Marcus woke with a start and sat upright in bed, his body soaked with sweat and his heart thudding from the dream that had held him captive.

He'd heard a thud.

He listened for it again, but it didn't come, and he quickly tore back the covers of his bed, got up and went through the house, waiting for her to appear, waiting for her to speak, waiting for that thud again.

But the shadows were all only dismal shadows, and the quiet was unpunctuated.

There was no one here.

Still, he knew he'd heard a thud, so he pulled down the steps to his attic, climbed up them and pulled the string that turned on the light.

It was dusty and musty smelling, but the chair he had moved up here last month looked inviting. He stooped across the floor until he reached it, then sat down and looked out the window at the lights on the porch fronts all around his neighborhood.

Nowhere else in the house could he have such a perspective, and that was why he'd entertained the idea of renting out rooms in his house to help him earn a living, making the attic his own room. But he'd abandoned that thought when the first of the prospective tenants had inspected the house and he'd realized instantly how unbearable it would be to share it with someone else. He needed his solitude, he'd admitted to himself finally. And even the attic wouldn't offer him enough.

But tonight, as he looked out on the loneliness of the street he lived on, he realized that solitude was the last thing he needed. He wanted to hear that thud again, that same thud that had led him to find her before, slumped on his floor, sick and disoriented.

He heard another thud and jumped. Suddenly a mouse ran across the floor. That was all it had been, he thought, his heart deflating. Just a mouse knocking a book off the stack where he had left it. Not a woman. Not Sarah.

A miserable dread climbed in his heart as he wondered when—or if—he would ever see her again.

The ballet recital in the fifth grade. Sarah sat up in bed, suddenly awakened from a restless sleep, and stared into the darkness, her heart pounding. He had been there. She remembered it now.

She'd had a special solo part in the recital and had danced her finest. And as she'd come forward for her final curtsy, the audience had cheered and whistled.

She had backed behind the curtain, allowing it to close, and when she'd left the stage he had been there, off to the side, like one of the congratulatory parents—only he'd been there for her.

She remembered the rose he had given her, a pure white rose, remembered that he'd smiled with misty eyes and told her that he felt the star of the show deserved something beautiful of her own.

She didn't even remember if she had said thank-you, for she'd been so surprised and so flattered. She had brought the rose to her face, closed her eyes as she breathed the scent. When she had opened them again, she'd seen only his back as he cut through the crowd of costumed dancers and left the backstage area.

It was Marcus. She knew it now, from the most certain depths of her consciousness. He had been watching her, probably as he'd done a hundred other times. Only his presence had never registered before now.

"I've got to get back to you, Marcus," she whispered as tears stung her eyes again. "I won't let you live your life watching a little girl grow up not knowing you."

She lay back down on the pillow, closed her eyes and tried to dream, again, of the man with the rose, the man with the balloon, the man who had held her and let her cry.

Tomorrow, she thought, just before sleep washed over her. Tomorrow she would see him again.

She phoned Caren first thing the next morning and laid the groundwork for her disappearing for a few days. "I'm going to Cancún to shoot the Bill Blass summer collection," she said. "I'll be gone a few days, and I'm not sure when I'll be back."

"Isn't this kind of sudden?" her sister asked. "I mean, you hadn't mentioned it at all."

"Yeah. Actually, it's a reshoot. They didn't like what we did in Bermuda, so we had to schedule it at the last minute."

Something about Caren's pause told Sarah she wasn't buying it. But how could she have expected otherwise? Since she was a little girl, Caren had somehow just known when things weren't right. And Sarah had known, too. She had known the moment Caren lost her virginity, even though her sister denied it. And when Sarah was sixteen and had her first wreck, Caren had known instantly and driven to the site.

"So...when did you say you'd be back?" The question was posed to trick her, but Sarah was ready.

"I told you, I'm not sure. It depends on how well it goes. I've cleared everything for next week, just to make sure."

"Uh-huh." Quiet again. "What if you get sick again, Sarah? It could come back, you know."

"I'm well, Caren. How many times do I have to tell you?"

"I guess you'll just have to prove it."

"I will. I'll come back from Cancún with a wonderful, healthy-looking tan, and you'll never doubt me again."

"Uh-huh. Well, okay. Have a good time in Cancún—or wherever it is you're really going."

Sarah smiled. Caren wasn't fooled, but she wasn't worried, either, and she supposed she'd been appeased enough to not show up and call out for her...call her back...until she'd had a little more time with Marcus.

"So how will I get in touch with you? In case of emergency, I mean?"

"I don't know where I'm going to be staying yet," she evaded.

"Then...would Mick be able to reach you?"

"Yeah...he'd know." The lie almost stuck in her throat, and she knew her sister sensed it. "Look, I have to go pack. I'll call you when I get back. I love you."

"I love you, too." Caren sounded hurt, as if she'd been left out of some part of her sister's life, some part she couldn't name but that she needed to share in, to approve of. "Be careful."

Sarah hung up the phone and stared at it for a long time. What was she doing? she asked herself. What if she did go back to Marcus, and got so involved with him that she had to make a choice? A choice between his time and hers. A choice between him and Caren.

And what if Caren *didn't* call her back? She would be caught there, in Marcus's time, and she'd never see her sister, the other part of herself, again. And Caren would grieve for her, wonder where she was, and probably never overcome her despair at not knowing what had happened.

But she would call, Sarah knew. And then she'd have to leave Marcus, who was fast becoming the life to fill the void in her soul. He had loved her all her life, had loved her even before she was born. He had watched her patiently, waiting for her to grow up, but by the time she had, he'd been a withered old man. And now he was dead. The thought that she would never feel his arms around her again, never make long, sweet love to him, never hear his voice in her ear...it was more than she could bear to imagine.

She had to go back, or let it end the way it had the first time. It was in her hands to change it. She really had no choice.

She changed into a soft sweater and skirt that hugged her knees, and surveyed her reflection in the mirror, wondering if she could pass for an authentic 1950s woman. Deciding that the look was close enough, she went to the camera, which was still set up on the tripod where she had left it before, set the timer and took her place on the stool. As she waited, she tried to concentrate on Marcus, his face when he found her again, his joy at having her back.

When the jolt hit her this time, knocking her to the floor, she held on tight and tried to remember that the violent illness drawing her under would pass soon enough.

He found her heaped on the floor in his dining room again, unconscious and white as a ghost. Falling beside her, he gathered her into his arms. "My God," he whispered. "You're back."

Her breathing was unsteady, and quickly he ran to the medical bag he hadn't opened in months, got out a syringe and gave her a shot of aspirin, not certain whether it would help. Ice, he thought. He needed ice, and some oxygen to help her breathe, and some penicillin in case some infection was raging through her blood.

Damn it, he thought. He needed a hospital. But if he took her there, how could he explain where she'd come from? And what if taking her out of this house caused some problem in the whole paradoxical event, forcing her back before she even found consciousness?

He ran into the living room, picked up the telephone and dialed Gene's number.

"Hello?"

"Gene, it's me. Mark."

"Yeah. It's the middle of the night, man. What's up?"

"Sorry to wake you, but I've got an emergency. I need your help."

"Sure, man. What?"

"I need some ice. Lots of it. And some penicillin and an IV."

"What's going on, man?"

"Just..." He glanced back over his shoulder, desperate to hurry back to her. "Please, Gene. Can you help me or not?"

"Well, I have penicillin here, and I could get the ice and stuff at the hospital. Are you sick?"

"Not me. Somebody else."

"So take 'em to the hospital."

"Can't," he said. "Please, Gene. Just do it and don't say anything. Can I count on you?"

"Of course, man. I'll be there as soon as I can."

Marcus hung up, dashed back into the bedroom and stared at her colorless face. He went into the bathroom, threw all of his towels into the shower, turned it on and soaked them with cold water. Then he took them back to her, covering her with them.

But it wasn't long until they were warm from the heat of her skin.

The doorbell rang within half an hour, and Marcus ran to open it. Gene stood there with six bags of crushed ice on a dolly, an IV pole and a bag full of medicines he'd gotten from the hospital.

"Thanks, man. I owe you one," Marcus said, taking the dolly and pole from him and wheeling it into the house. It left a trail of water on the hardwood floor, but he ignored it.

"Anything I can do?" Gene asked. "Maybe you need another opinion."

"No," he said. "I know what to do."

"I thought you'd quit practicing," Gene said, in almost a taunting tone.

"I don't have time for this right now," Marcus said. "Sorry I woke you, and like I said, I owe you one."

He opened the door for Gene to go out, and the man only frowned darkly at him. "You're sure everything's okay?"

"It will be," Marcus said.

Gene went through the door and turned back at the steps of the porch. "Call me again if you need me, okay? I'll do whatever I can."

"Right." He didn't wait for Gene to be all the way down the steps before he closed the door and took the ice to his bed.

Quickly he packed her in the ice, then searched for a vein and started the IV drip.

Then all that was left to do was wait until she opened her eyes, became herself again and let him hold her so tight that she could never disappear from his grip again.

It was hours before she woke, hours of Marcus keeping worried vigil beside her, hours of wet towels and melting ice around her to break the fever, hours of fearing that she wouldn't wake at all.

Then, finally, her eyes opened, and he lurched forward. "Sarah?"

It took a moment for her eyes to focus on him, and he stroked her hair back from her face. Her forehead was cool, but she still looked as pale as death. "Mark?"

"How do you feel?" he asked quietly.

"Not good." She tried to sit up, but she was too weak. "Bedpan," she whispered.

He gave her the bedpan and, turning on her side, she retched into it. Patiently he stroked her hair, wiped her face, uttered gentle, comforting words as she threw up.

Finally she dropped back onto the pillow. "How long have I been like this?"

"Five, six hours," he said. "Much longer than last time, and you aren't through it yet."

"I guess it gets worse each time," she whispered. "My body gets weaker or something."

"Each time what?" he asked.

She closed her eyes and shook her head, for she was too weak, too dizzy, to tell him everything just yet. When she opened her eyes again, he was staring at her with tormented eyes, eyes that couldn't tolerate another moment of patience.

"Sarah, I have to know," he whispered. "Are you a ghost?"

"No," she said.

"Then . . . are you some retribution from God? My punishment? My hell?"

Her face contorted, she shook her head, with more vigor than she'd had since she awoke. "No."

His eyes began to burn with unspent tears, and his expression was more tortured than any she'd ever seen.

"Then, in God's name, tell me where you came from and why you've chosen me to torment."

Tears sprang to her eyes, and she struggled to sit up, to look at him, to make him understand. There was no holding back, she told herself. She didn't know how much time she had, but it wasn't enough. It would never be enough. It was time to tell him everything and suffer the consequences of his disbelief, whatever they were.

She cleared her throat and wiped her eyes. "You see, Marcus . . . there was this old man. . . ."

And, as chronologically as she could, since time was such an inaccurate concept, she told him the whole story.

His face looked as pale as hers when she finished her story and allowed silence to seep between them. Struggling to grasp the unreality of what she had told him, he got up and paced across the room, leaned against the mantel, then turned back and sought her with eyes that couldn't believe—but did, anyway.

"If all this is true," he said in a hoarse voice, "why would you come back here, knowing how ill it makes you?"

She was silent for a moment, mulling over the question herself. Her eyes locked with his, the softest, saddest, most tragic eyes she had ever seen. "Because I wanted to know you."

Down the hall she heard the cuckoo clock sounding 3:00 a.m. and the little Dutch girl spinning around in a circle to its staccato tune. Marcus came toward her, reached out for her face with gentle, tentative fingers. "I wouldn't believe a word of this," Marcus whispered, "except that I've seen you disappear myself. It must be true." He sat down beside her, rubbing his face.

"It is true, Marcus. I couldn't make this up."

Silence rippled between them for another eternity as he gazed at her in amazement.

"So you're telling me that the minute your sister calls for you you'll start to fade back through time?"

"That's right," she whispered. "But I tried to take care of it by telling her I'd be out of town. In a few days, she'll check out my story with Mick and realize I lied, so she'll come by the house, find my car in the garage and assume I'm home. She'll call out for me, and I'll fade back."

"So how long does that leave us?"

"I don't know," she whispered. "It seems like a lot more time passes here than it does there. When I go back, it's later than it was when I left, but not as much time has passed."

"Then you could be called back anytime?"

"I suppose so," she whispered. "I hope I have at least enough time to recover from this before I have to go through it all again."

His eyebrows furrowed closer together. "You're like this on the return trip? This sick?"

"Yes. Last time Caren found me unconscious and called an ambulance. They couldn't find what was wrong with me, and finally the symptoms vanished."

Marcus's face twisted in horror. "My God, Sarah, don't you see what you're doing? You're getting sicker and sicker each time. What if no one finds you the next time?"

"Caren will, because I can't go back without her calling me. It's okay, Marcus. Really."

"But, Sarah, you can't keep putting your body through this kind of trauma. Your organs are growing weaker each time, and before long they'll stop functioning entirely."

"I can't help it." Tears edged her eyes again. "I had to come back. I couldn't let it end that way." She reached out for him in agonized longing, tears rolling down her face. He leaned over her, and she touched his face with trembling hands. "Don't you see, Marcus? In my time, you're dead now. You spent your life watching me, waiting for me to grow up, only to die before we ever met."

"There are worse things."

"What?" she asked, almost angry at the suggestion. "Name one."

"You dying before you've even reached the age I am now. Dying because of some phenomenon that neither of us understands."

"But I'm not dying," she said. "I'm fine. I'm feeling better already. The symptoms are almost gone."

He looked down into her hopeful face. It was so open and expressive, so optimistic in a time when only the worst kind of pessimism was called for. He slid his arms around her, crushed her against him and held her for the rest of the morning. She fell asleep in his arms, slept like a baby wrapped in protective arms.

And he knew that if he had the choice, he'd sit right here with her, like this, for the rest of his life.

CHAPTER SEVEN

She was well when she woke this time, and Marcus saw instantly that the color had returned to her skin, and the life sparkled back in her eyes.

She looked up at him with sleepy eyes and smiled. "I'm still here," she whispered.

"Yes, you are," he said. "Thank God, you're still here."

His kiss cherished her, the way she'd always heard a man should cherish a woman. It was sweet, unhurried, but as intense as a simmering volcano that would erupt at the slightest provocation.

And Sarah offered him that provocation.

Their lovemaking was as explosive and as intense as if they knew, without a doubt, that there would never be another time for them to be together, another chance to fall in love, another shot at the sweet delirium they had each waited a lifetime to find.

Afterward, they lay together on sheets that were still wet from melted ice, and Marcus stroked his hand over her breasts, her stomach, the tops of her thighs. "You're so beautiful," he whispered. "Do the men in your time realize that?"

She smiled. "The men in my time...they aren't like you, Marcus."

He propped himself on one elbow and looked down at her. "Tell me about them."

"Well, they're ruined, sort of. Women's lib confused them...."

"Women's lib?"

"Oh, yeah. That doesn't come for a few more years," she said. "Women's liberation. It's when women rise up and fight for equal rights. Equal pay, equal opportunity, equal representation. They'll be burning their bras."

He grinned. "Now there's something to look forward to."

"But it's serious," she said. "It's a pivotal point in history. Women will start taking themselves more seriously as human beings. And the men have to relearn everything."

"You don't sound like you think this is such a bad idea."

"I don't. It's wonderful. In my time, we have women in key cabinet positions, women in congress, women as governors, lawyers, doctors."

"So what's the problem with the men?"

"Because we've turned into these tough, independent fighters, our men don't know how to treat us anymore," she said on a sigh. "They don't know whether to open our door for us, slide out our chair, pay for a meal on a date.... And all the chivalry's gone. All that's left is one-night stands and a lot of lines that don't mean anything anymore."

"Oh, come on. You probably have all sorts of suitors. How many marriage proposals have you had?"

She smiled. "Oh, Marcus, it's not like that in my time. Marriage is the last thing most of the men I meet want. And if I'm not willing to play by their loose little rules, then they move on to someone who will."

"Surely there must be some decent men. Men who see the value in someone like you."

"My sister found one like that," she said, smiling wistfully. "Jimmy. The love of her life. If I thought there were two like him, I'd search the world over. But I'm not real optimistic."

"So you traveled back forty-some years to find one?"

"Something like that," she said.

His smile faded, and he touched her face, stroked a knuckle over her jawline. "When you go back," he whispered, "I want you to be happy. I want you to find someone who can cherish you."

She closed her eyes and clutched his hand to her face, and tears seeped from under her lashes. "I want it to be you."

"But that can't be," he whispered.

He kissed her again, and their tongues swirled and mated with the heartfelt despair of time-crossed lovers. When the kiss broke, they clung to one another, as if they'd known each other for years, as if neither could imagine life without the other, as if time were some monster that would snatch them apart without a second's notice.

Finally he pulled away from her, went across the room and withdrew a camera from his drawer. "Is this the camera?"

She caught her breath. "Yes! Marcus, that's it!"

"I wonder..." His eyes grew wide at the idea forming in his brain. "Let's think about this for a minute. If this is the camera you found...and it brought you here...maybe it could transport me to your time."

"But what if it didn't?" she asked. "I didn't set a timer, or tell it where to put me. What if it sent you back? What if it dropped you into some other time? And who would call you back?"

"You," he said. "You could call me back if I went wrong."

"But it doesn't work for just anyone. My sister's my twin. We've always had a kind of telepathy between us. What if I hadn't been a twin? I've thought about this, and I'm not sure if anyone else could have ever done it. It's too complicated, Marcus. You could wind up in some godforsaken time, and I would never find you again."

"You found me this time. Fate planned this, Sarah. It was meant to happen."

"Maybe so, Marcus, but we're not talking about climbing mountains or swimming oceans to find each other. If you go back instead of forward, how will I ever find you? You'll be lost to me forever. And if you go forward too far, will I have to grow old to be with you this time?"

He set the camera down and lowered back onto the bed next to her. His face was sober, strained, as he gazed down at her. "Do you know what it did to me when you disappeared through my fingers?"

She swallowed. "I think so."

"I felt toyed with, like God had dangled happiness in my face, then snatched it away before I could claim it."

Her hand came up to touch his face. "I'm sorry, Marcus."

"And now," he went on, his voice wavering with the emotion rippling on it, "to have you here again, to show me colors when I had gotten used to living in a gray world... I can't just watch you slip away again, without trying to find some way..."

"I'll come back," she cut in with earnest certainty.

"But when? How many more times? What will it do to you?"

"It doesn't matter," she whispered. "I'll come."

He pulled her into a desperate embrace and held her so tightly that for an instant she allowed herself to believe that nothing, not even time, could draw them apart. "I want you with me all the time," he said. "I don't care where we are, or when. But I want us together.

"We have to try to find a way," he said. "That's why we have to experiment with the camera. Maybe we could try to send something else back—an object— and see if you find it when you go back."

She thought about that for a moment. "Yes, it could work, I guess."

"Tell me," he said, opening the camera and finding it empty. "Do you wind up in the same room you started out in?"

"Yes," she said.

"Then we'll send something, and you'll know to look for it there. If it works, you can send it back to me. And that's how I'll know that I can come to you."

She caught her breath as tears filled her eyes. "Oh, Marcus, it would be so wonderful. But what if no one's here to call you back?"

"That's the beauty of it," he said. "No one is close enough to me to call. So I'd have to stay there."

"But so many things have changed, Marcus. It's not the same world."

"It would be fascinating," he said. "And I'd experience it all with you."

Delighted with the possibility, she threw her arms around him, and as they began to make love again, this time with glorious delirium rather than tragic ambition, she realized that—just maybe—there was hope here, after all.

Later that afternoon, after Marcus had showered and shaved and emerged from the bedroom in a sport shirt and dark plaid trousers, he pulled Sarah onto his lap. "How would you feel about leaving the house?" he asked. "We need to buy film so we can test our theory, but I don't want to leave you here alone."

A shadow of fear fell over her face. "I don't know. What if someone sees me?"

"It'll be okay. If we run into anyone I know, I'll tell them you're visiting from out of town."

She considered it for a moment, but the fear was too great. "I don't know how to act in the fifties, Mark.

I'd give myself away. My clothes aren't quite right, and I don't know how to do those hairstyles...."

"Your clothes could have come from the store down the street," he said. "And you don't have to wear a beehive just to go to the drugstore."

"But what if I get called back and someone sees me disappear?"

"Worse than that," Marcus said, "what if you get called back while I'm not here? I couldn't stand coming home and not finding you."

She sighed. "We really need that film, don't we?"

"We really do," he said. "Besides, you said yourself that you didn't expect Caren to call you back for a few days. Maybe we're still pretty safe."

A slow smile tugged at her lips. "All right," she whispered. "I would kind of like to see what the town looks like now."

"I'd like to know how it's going to change," he said.

Marcus's car was a baby blue 1950 Chevrolet convertible, and he took a moment to put the top down as she got in. While she waited, she looked around at the neighborhood, which looked so different from the way it did in her time. The homes were small and sweet and neat, and housewives swept the front porches in pedal pushers or circular skirts, while children who looked no different from the ones in her own neighborhood dug in the dirt or rode tricycles on the sidewalks.

"Hi, Dr. Mark," a teenage girl called from a flower bed next door. "It's good to see you out."

Marcus smiled and lifted his hand in a wave. "How are you, Beth Ann?"

"I'm fine. Are the two of you going for a drive?"

He smiled, as if that were obvious, and said, "Thought we would."

"Have fun," she said.

He got into the car and backed out of the drive, and all the while the girl strained to see Sarah. Deliberately she diverted her face until they drove away. "She seemed awfully curious," she said. "Do you think she'll tell anyone she saw us?"

"Everybody she sees," he said with a smile. "Maybe it'll divert some of the talk about my turning into a recluse and giving up medicine. I'd imagine the town's having a field day with that."

"Now they'll be guessing about the mystery woman," she mused. "Stella had heard that I was a married woman."

"Stella?" he asked.

"Your future landlady," she said. "The one who gave me your things."

"Oh, yes," he said. "The closest person in the world to me. My landlady." The words were spoken sadly, as though the idea of dying so alone disturbed him. Sarah gazed at him, wishing from her soul that she could offer him some reassurance that things would change, but it was likely that she had only made things worse.

They turned the corner, leaving the neighborhood, and she saw a big pasture across the front, on which several horses grazed. "It's so different," she whispered. "In my time there's another whole neighborhood here, and over there a convenience store."

"What's that?"

"A little store where you can buy groceries for twice the price in half the time."

"So why not just go to a grocery store?"

"Because everybody's in a hurry. There's never any time." Her eyes drifted off down the street, searching for familiarity, but everything was different. "There's an apartment complex here—"

"A what?"

"Apartments. You know. A building that has a lot of apartments where people live. And that gas station...it isn't there. It must have been torn down." She smiled at the little gas station, with a man who looked like Gomer Pyle chatting with a customer while he washed his windshield.

They turned the corner again, and she caught her breath as the small church that still stood in her time caught her eye. "Oh, my gosh! The church!"

He glanced over at it. "You recognize it?"

"Yes. Only in my time, it's boarded up and rotting. They'll tear it down soon, but, oh, isn't it beautiful now?"

"My parents are buried in the graveyard behind it," he said. "And I was baptized there. I haven't darkened its doors in two and a half years, though."

"Oh, do you think we could go in it later? Just so I could see the inside?"

"Sure," he said. "But first let's get the film."

They came to the bridge, which seemed unaltered from her time, and she smiled. "The bridge. I have to cross it to get to my sister's house. It looks just the same."

She glanced over at him and saw that he was watching her with a sweet, awestruck look in his eyes. "What?"

"Do you know how beautiful you are?" he whispered. "With that look in your eye and that sweet expression on your face?"

She felt the pink rising up her cheeks, and pushed her hair back from her face. "It's just all so much slower, neater, sweeter now than it becomes later. I would like to have lived now."

"You are living now," he pointed out.

"Yeah," she whispered, "but I wish it weren't just temporary."

He pulled the car over beside the bridge and got out, then came around to her side and opened her door. Taking her hand, he pulled her out, and they walked up on the bridge and looked out over the river. "I wish it weren't temporary, either," he said. "I wish you could stay here and grow old with me. Fill up all my hours, busy all my thoughts, give me something stronger than the past to focus on."

Tears came to her eyes, but she looked into the wind as it whipped her hair back from her face. "Oh, look, Mark. From right here, if I look straight out over the river and not left or right, it looks just like my time. Wouldn't it be wonderful if we could stand here like this, side by side in the same time, knowing that neither of us would vanish into thin air? Wouldn't that be great?''

He pulled her into his arms and held her with fierce longing, with tragic intensity. Several cars passed, and a bicyclist pedaled by, but they didn't draw apart. Finally he pulled back, wiped his eyes and whispered, ''Come on.''

CHAPTER EIGHT

They drove to the Walgreens, and she went inside with him. The store looked like a museum of old ads and products, and she looked around her, taking it all in. The smell of ice cream and malts wafted over the air, and she saw the soda fountain in the back. "Strangers in Paradise" played over a transistor radio in the back, and hanging on the wall was a big Coca-Cola ad claiming it was "The Pause that Refreshes."

He bought several boxes of film and a pack of cigarettes, and looking over his shoulder, she asked, "You smoke?"

"Sometimes," he said.

She waited until he'd finished paying and turned back to her before saying, "It'll give you lung cancer, you know. The surgeon general has a warning label on every pack in my time," she whispered.

"And people still smoke?"

"Well, yes..."

He went to a trash can, dropped the pack in. "I won't smoke anymore, okay? Does that make you feel better?"

Her smile was soft as she felt her temper settling again. "Much."

He laughed. "Good. Come on, I'll buy you a soda."

"Sure, why not?"

He took her back and ordered one malted with two straws, and together they sat sipping and smiling at each other. "I feel like something out of a Norman Rockwell painting. You know, these soda fountains aren't in style anymore in my day. Now everything's fast food...hamburgers and french fries made to order. You can drive up to the window, get your food and eat it in the car as you drive to the gym to do aerobics."

He shook his head. "It's like another language, you know."

She smiled. "I know. Aerobics is an exercise class done to music on CDs."

"What's a CD?"

"It's a record, only instead of wax, it's metal."

"You mean, no more LPs and 45s?"

"They went out of style in the early eighties."

He laughed again, and she realized how rare it was for him. The naturalness of it struck her, and she smiled poignantly.

"What else do you want to know?"

"Who's going to win the fight between Roland LaStarza and Rocky Marciano?"

Sarah laughed. "Heck if I know."

"Darn," he said, snapping his fingers. "I thought I could make some money on that."

Something told her Marcus hadn't cracked a joke in a very long time, and as she smiled at him, she wondered why. The spirit she saw in him now wasn't entirely buried, yet she knew it would be eventually.

He reached across her and picked up a newspaper someone had left on the counter. "We'll take this home if you want, so you can read it and scoff and laugh at how backward we are."

She glanced at the front page and saw Richard Nixon and Dwight Eisenhower shaking hands with the chairman of the House Ways and Means Committee. "Oh, my gosh. Nixon's vice president, isn't he?"

He shot her a look. "What about it?"

"He'll be president later. Congress will take a vote to impeach him, but he'll resign before they can."

"Why? He's the best veep we've ever had."

"Dirty politics," she said. "Putting himself above the law. And lying through his teeth. But that's twenty years away yet. Oh, look! John and Jackie are getting married!"

He shrugged and tossed the paper down. "If you ask me, that's a lot of stuff about nothing."

"Not really," she said, picking the paper up again and reading about the wedding. "In less than ten years, he's going to be president. And he'll be assassinated in a Dallas parade."

Marcus gave her a stricken look. "I don't think I want to know this stuff. Some of it's a little disturbing."

"Yeah," she whispered. "I guess it would be."

He looked at her for a moment, his face thoughtful. "I wonder...if this works, and my camera can get us both back to your time, how will I ever get caught up? I'll be perceived as stupid. Nothing will be the same."

"I'll teach you," she said. "It's not that hard. You'll soak it all up."

"Still..."

His hesitancy deflated her spirits somewhat, and she looked into his eyes. "It's an awful lot to ask of you, Marcus. You'd be giving up everything...starting over completely."

He looked down at the bag of film, then back to her. "But the alternative is out of the question."

They both knew what that alternative was, and the emptiness it would create in both their souls. He took her hand, squeezed it, then brought it to his lips.

"You know," she whispered, "if you wanted to practice medicine, you'd probably have to go back to school...."

"No," he whispered, looking down at the soda. "I told you, I can't do that again."

"Not even in my time?" she asked.

"Not ever," he said. "Some people are meant to be healers. Some aren't. It's a privilege that can be taken away."

He slid off his stool and laid some money down on the counter. "Come on. We have to get home."

She followed him quietly, and when they were back **in his** car she touched his arm, tried to say something that would change his mood back to the one she had glimpsed over that soda. But, not knowing what had triggered the change, she couldn't find the words. "Marcus, I'm sorry."

He laid his hand over hers. "No, I'm sorry. You didn't say anything wrong."

The breeze swept through his hair, ruffling it and making his eyes look paler and more vulnerable. "I want to know you," she whispered.

"I know," he said. "It's just...not easy to talk about." He started the car and drove back to his house. As they went inside, she felt a sense of anticipation in the air, as if he was working through the words he would use to tell her the darkest secret of his life.

He tossed his keys on the table beside the door and watched her go to the couch to sit down. "If you really want to know about me...about why I quit medicine," he whispered, "I'll tell you."

"I do," she said. "What would make a man give up something he obviously put so much time and effort into?"

"Failure," he said. He sat down and leaned forward, set his elbows on his knees and stared down at the floor. "You can't have any idea how many lives I failed to save over there. How many mothers grieved, how many sisters and wives were heartbroken because I had to make a choice to save one man and not another."

"But that couldn't have been your fault."

"I wasn't fast enough, I wasn't wise enough, I made mistakes, I let people die."

"But how many did you save?"

He looked up at her. "A lot. But it's the ones I didn't save who haunt me at night...."

His voice faded out, and she touched his arm. "Marcus, in about ten years we're going to go to war again, only this time it's in Vietnam. It's going to be a terrible, bloody, pointless war, even worse than Korea, if you could imagine that. And a lot of men are going to come home tragically affected by what they'll see there. There's a term, Post Traumatic Stress Disorder, that psychiatrists use to describe the depression you've been feeling. It's normal, but you can get help."

"Where?" he asked. "You want me to go to a shrink, lie on some couch and talk about my childhood and my sexual fantasies?"

"No," she whispered. "You need to go and talk about what you saw there. How it changed you. The guilt you're carrying around. A good doctor can help you."

"There isn't a doctor alive who sat out the war in a nice, clean office who could understand the true depth of my guilt," he said, his voice breaking. "Don't you understand? When I first saw you disappear, I was sure you were the ghost of a sister or wife of one of the men whose blood I had on my hands, one of the men who looked up at me, begging with their eyes for me to save them, only I couldn't...."

"But now you know I'm not your retribution, Marcus. Now you know I'm not punishment for something that was out of your control."

"Plenty was in my control," he said.

"What was? That people came to you almost dead, and you couldn't bring them back?"

"You don't know everything," he said. "I can't tell you everything. You just...you can never understand. And as for your being my retribution, all I know for sure is that I grow old waiting for you, and I die before I ever look into your eyes again. You don't think that's a hell all its own?"

There was nothing more she could say, so instead she raised up on her knees, put her arms around him and held him as he had held her when she'd wept that first time.

They made love with sweet, tragic languor; it was a bonding kind of lovemaking that would forever brand each of their signatures on the other's soul, a merging of spirits that could never be separated again. Not even through decades and generations of time.

Afterward they lay in each other's arms, and Marcus whispered, "Let's try the camera. See if there's any way to work this out."

So they got up and dressed, got the film loaded, then looked around for the perfect object to send. "It has to be something that wouldn't normally be there," she said. "So we can be sure."

He scanned the objects in his home, and his eyes landed on the chess set in the corner of the room. "The chess set," he said. "It has my name engraved on the back."

"All right," she said. "Let's try it."

They each held their breath as Sarah took the camera, held it to her eye and clicked.

There was no jolt this time and when she lowered the camera, she saw that the chess set hadn't moved.

"What happened?" he asked.

"Nothing," she said, "other than a pretty boring picture of a chess set."

"Try something smaller." He found her a little figurine of a kitten a patient had given him. "Here, try this."

Concentrating, she focused the camera and clicked the shutter. "Still nothing," she said when the figurine stayed in place.

Marcus dropped down onto the sofa. "Then I don't understand. You're sure it's the same camera?"

"Well, it looks like it, and I found it in the attic. It was so old, it's a wonder it worked at all."

"But if it had some power, why wouldn't it have it now?"

"Who knows?" she asked, sinking down beside him. "The fact that it works in the first place is unexplainable. Even ludicrous. But it does."

For a moment, they sat staring at the camera, quietly contemplating the possibilities that had just died a quiet death. Then something sparked back to life, and Marcus looked at her. "What if it only works on people? You've taken other pictures with it in your time, and I've taken pictures here, too. Nothing was ever transported before. Not until you."

She met his eyes, saw the intention there, and wondered if they were about to make a bigger mess of the fate that was already hopelessly twisted. "There's no way to test it," she whispered. "We just have to do it, don't we?"

"Together," he said. "We'll set the timer to photograph us together. And wherever—whenever—we wind up, we'll be there together."

She took his hand, her eyes poignantly soft as she looked up at him. "Are you sure, Marcus?"

"Yes," he said without hesitation. "Are you?"

"Caren will probably call me back from wherever I am." Tears filled her eyes, and she said, "But what about you? I'm just so afraid..."

"Don't be afraid," he said. "It'll be okay. We have to try. You know we do."

She nodded quietly and watched him set the camera on a table, get them into focus and set the timer. He came back to her as the time ticked by, set his arm around her shoulders, held her tightly against him.

"If it doesn't work," he whispered as the time ticked down, "at least I'll have a remembrance of you. Of us. And if it does, we'll have the rest of our lives."

Hope took flight in her heart as the last few seconds ticked by, and she held her breath as the flash bulb clicked.

But there was no jolt, and they were still here, with his furnishings, in his house, in his time....

"It didn't work," she whispered as a sob rose to her throat. "Oh, Marcus. It didn't work."

Masking his own defeat, he pulled her into an embrace and held her for a long, quiet moment, and finally he whispered, "Do you believe in God?"

"Yes," she said. "I do. Do you?"

"Yes," he whispered. "But sometimes I think he's an angry God, merciless and cruel. Why else would things work out the way they do?"

"Maybe those aren't things He's done. Maybe, instead, He tries to set them right after they've gone wrong."

"Do you believe in destiny?"

"Yes." She looked up at him, saw his eyes focused on something she couldn't see, something his mind was working out.

"Do you believe that God works sometimes to fulfill destiny? Maybe in mysterious, unbelievable ways?"

"I do now," she said.

"Then maybe—if you're right, and He is a God of mercy—maybe we're meant to be together," he whispered. "But by some fluke, one of us wound up in the wrong time. What if God is just trying to set things right?"

She looked up at him. "Do you think there's a chance it could be set right?" she asked. "That I won't be called back? That I could stay here with you?"

"Do you want to?" he asked, sitting up straighter and looking down at her. "Do you really want to?"

Tears burst into her eyes, and she shook her head. "I don't know, Marcus. I don't know if I could face never seeing my sister again. We're twins, and I couldn't imagine being closer to anyone in the world. Besides, I'd always be on guard, waiting for her to call me back, constantly expecting to disappear. How could I live like that?"

Marcus laid his head back on the couch and looked up at the ceiling. "I guess you'd have to find a way to keep her from doing that. Maybe tell her the truth. But then you'd have to choose." A moment of thick silence stretched between them. "Which would you choose, Sarah?"

She looked over at him, noted the pain in his eyes, the love on his face, and she had no doubt at all. "Caren has Jimmy," she whispered. "And now I have you."

"Then we have to find a way," he said. "We have to find some way that we can each live the rest of our lives in the same time."

"We will," she whispered. "I think the first time it didn't end right. I think I must have come to you that first time, then disappeared, and you literally waited for me to be born and grow up. It was like a circle, my coming back here, your growing old, dying, then my finding the camera, coming back for the first time all over again..."

"Only this time it's going to end differently."

"This visit didn't happen the first time," she said. "What if my coming this second time has already changed things? What if we really could make it end differently?"

His eyes filled as he beheld her, and he touched her face with the gentlest caress she'd ever felt. "I have to believe that," he whispered. "I don't think I could stand it if I didn't."

"I'll think of something," she said. "Trust me, Marcus. I promise I'll think of something."

That night, as darkness fell, Marcus became restless and nervous, as if he was waiting for her to vanish from his embrace at any moment. His anticipation of that made it impossible for them to relax.

"Let's go out," he said finally. "I want you to have something to remember, something more than the same walls you see all the time, anyway."

"I have plenty to remember," she said.

"But this house can be pretty dismal twenty-four hours a day. We'll drive downtown and go for a walk. No place real public. It might be dangerous to sit in a restaurant and risk your fading away."

"What if you see people you know?"

"Then the gossip will be all over town by morning. But it's okay. It'll divert the talk about how I've gone insane."

She smiled a weak smile, but something in her heart twisted at the seriousness with which he said it. There was more to his story about Korea, she thought, and he wasn't going to tell her. What could it be, she wondered, that he had locked himself in this house, alienating everyone who knew him?

For the first time, it occurred to her that maybe God had sent her to save him. Maybe she was the one chance he had to pull out of the mire of his depression.

He waited while she put her hair up, and she almost wished she had some makeup, some lipstick or eye shadow, though she rarely wore it. Still, she wanted tonight to be special. She wanted him to remember her, too, as the beautiful woman who had touched his life. For, despite her promises and all their precarious plans, she knew she might never get back to him again.

When she was ready, he stepped into the living room, where he waited in pressed trousers and a white shirt. The look on his face was more tragic than approving. "You're so beautiful," he whispered.

She smiled. "I don't really know how to do that beehive stuff with my hair, but I did the best I could."

"I'm so proud of you," he said. "I wish I could show you off to everyone. But I can't...."

She reached up for him, pressed a kiss to his chin. "Tonight, let's just pretend that we're normal lovers on a date. That time isn't ticking by, waiting to drag us apart. Tonight, let's pretend we have forever on our side. Maybe we really do."

He swallowed the emotions he was struggling with and took her hand. And as they left the house, she allowed herself to forget the madness that had brought her here. Tonight was for them, and no one—except Caren—could take it away from them.

CHAPTER NINE

Marcus parked his car in a space on Main Street, and they got out and held hands as they strolled past shop windows. A bingo game was in session at the VA hall, and players came and went in front of them. They passed a barber shop, where four old men were playing cards at a table, and, farther down, a café where young people on dates laughed and mingled to the sounds blaring from the jukebox.

They came to a Coke machine that looked to Sarah like an antique, and Sarah stopped and looked up at him, her eyes animated. "Marcus, is Coca-Cola really only a nickel?"

"Yep."

"Wow."

"How much is it in your time?"

"At least fifty cents, if you luck out and find one of the older machines. I buy it in the two-liter bottles, but..." She realized she was losing him, and she shook her head. "Never mind. You would think everything's outrageously expensive. I probably paid twenty times more for my house than you did."

He frowned. "Just you, alone? How did you afford it?"

The color climbed into her cheeks again. "I make a pretty good living."

"As a photographer?"

"Yeah," she said. "I'm kind of in demand. I'm good."

His appreciative smile warmed her. "You're an interesting person."

"How do you mean?"

"I mean, you seem so confident. So independent. The women I worked with in Korea were like that, but there don't seem to be any of them around here."

"There will be," she said. "Boy, will there ever be. It's almost a shame."

"Why would you say that?"

"Because. A lot of women are going to have to go to work for economic reasons when they'd rather be home with their children. And those who do stay home are going to get a lot of flak for not working. Children are going to spend most of their time in day-care centers, then come home at night and park in front of the television until they go to bed, because their parents are too stressed out and too busy to play with them."

"Stressed out. That's a strange way of putting it." He frowned. "I don't think I'd like your time very much."

"No, you probably wouldn't," she whispered. Her heart seemed to sink with her words. "It's not all bad, though," she said. "There are good things about my time."

He stopped and pulled her into the doorway of a closed dress shop and slipped his arms around her. "Tell me what they are."

This close to him, wrapped in the safety of his arms, she found it hard to think. "Uh...well..." His eyes were the clearest blue, so pure and sweet that they made her want to forsake the people around them and kiss him until her lips hurt.

He kissed her, then pulled back, trying to look interested. "Really. I want to know."

"Good things." She struggled to think. "Well, my sister. She's great. I don't know what life would be like without her."

"What else?"

"Well, the opportunities women have. I can achieve whatever I want to...." Her eyes strayed to a dress on a mannequin in the window, and she shook her head. "Thing is, I'd give it all up if I just had someone of my own. Sometimes I think I keep so busy just because there are so many empty places in my life."

"Does your work fill them up?"

"No," she whispered, meeting his eyes again. "The only thing I've ever found to fill it up is you."

His kiss was tender, poignant, sweet in its demands, and she felt her bones turning to liquid and melting into her bloodstream. He was so big, she thought, and he made her feel so little. And not even the greatest sense of independence in the world could top that cared-for feeling.

Up the street, the sound of a piano spilled out of the doors of a restaurant, and Marcus took her hand again and pulled her back to the sidewalk. "Come on," he said. "We're going to dance."

She smiled up at him, completely trusting, yet worried at the risk they were taking. "Are we going in there?"

"No," he said. "Don't worry. There's a courtyard in the back, overlooking the river."

They passed the restaurant and went around to the back. As he had promised, a brick courtyard beckoned with soft lighting and the sound of the piano tinkling out from the restaurant. He stopped and turned to face her, brought her hand to his heart and pulled her against him.

Quietly, softly, slowly they danced, gazing into eyes that knew the tragedy of the separation that awaited them. Neither of them could smile any longer. There was too much at stake. Two hearts that were about to break.

"Why can't it be forever?" she whispered.

He couldn't answer, so instead he pulled her head against his chest, held her with the strength and commitment of a man who had no choice. After a moment, he released her, and she looked up at him again.

He struggled with words that weren't easy to utter, and she saw the intention in his eyes, the blue-hot need to express what was in his heart. "When you go back," he whispered, "remember that a man once loved you with his entire heart and soul. That you brought color back into his life and gave him a reason to grow old. Even if he had to do it without you."

Tears welled up in her eyes, spilled over onto her cheeks, and she saw the trembling in his lips, the mistiness in his eyes. With a shaky hand, she reached up and touched his face. "I love you, too, Marcus," she whispered. "And when I'm gone, I want you to remember that there was once a woman who fought and struggled her way through time just to be with you for a little while. No matter what happens, I'll never forget you."

"I don't want you to forget me," he whispered, "but I don't want you alone, either. I want you to find someone who can love you in the right time and place. I want you to feel how special you are...all the time."

"I can't imagine myself with anyone else."

"I can't, either," he said. "But I can't bear to imagine you in that big, dark house all alone, either."

She caught her breath on a sob and tried to curb her tears. But she had little control over them. "It's not worth talking about," she said. "Because I'll come back. No matter how many times Caren calls me home, I'll come back. As long as I've got that camera, you can always count on that."

He pulled her against him again, holding her with the force of his affection for her, and began to move to the music again. But somehow, as she laid her head against his chest, wishing there were some way to get even closer, she knew that Marcus no longer believed in happily-ever-afters.

They strolled back up the opposite side of the street, which was growing quieter as the night grew older. They held hands as they strolled past the movie theater, where *Roman Holiday,* with Audrey Hepburn, was playing. "You want to see a movie?" he asked.

She smiled. "I've seen that one three times."

"Have you? You mean they still play it?"

"Yeah," she said. "It's on video." She smiled when he shot her another questioning look. "You can rent movies to show on your own television. It's a whole new industry."

"But what's the fun of watching them at home?"

"Exactly."

"So do they still have theaters?"

"Of course," she said, "but there are ten or fifteen screens sometimes in one theater."

"Are there that many movies?"

"Yeah. Hollywood's as prolific as ever."

He brought her hand to his lips, kissed it as they walked. "So who do you go to these multimovies with?"

"Only one at a time," she told him. "And I go with different people."

"Do you have a lot of dates?"

"I date some," she said noncommittally. "No melding of the minds, if that's what you mean."

"How about sex?"

She shot a look to him, and grinned. "No, actually. I don't sleep with men I'm not in love with."

"But do they try?"

"They come on to me from time to time…but they know what their chances are."

"So why did you sleep with me?" He had stopped walking, and was gazing down at her, his eyes serious.

"Because it didn't seem real. It was crazy. Like none of my rules applied."

Satisfied, he smiled, and took her hand again. "I love you, Sarah," he whispered. "Thank you for coming back this second time."

They began walking again, and when they reached the car, he opened her door and helped her inside. They were quiet as they drove home, too quiet, and something worrisome began to stir inside Sarah. What if she went back and something prevented her from returning again? What if he continued hiding from his medical calling, continued to sit in darkness, like a hermit afraid the light might reveal too much?

She wanted more for him, and yet she knew it would take time to coax him out of his rejection of medicine. And time was something she just didn't have.

When they were back in his house, locked in the privacy of their own world outside time or space, outside reality and logic, he kissed her with the fierceness of a man deprived of a human touch for too long. They made love with almost dangerous abandon, intense, almost vicious love, as powerful and forceful on her part as on his. The peak of their loving was so explosive, so shattering, that they fluttered back down together, and, overwhelmed by the intensity of it all, Sarah started to cry.

Without a word, he held her for what seemed an eternity, without an interruption or a wayward thought, only that sweet melding of minds and souls, as sweet and bonding as the melding of their bodies had been.

When her tears were spent, she looked up at him, adoring his face with her fingertips. "Marcus, I need something from you," she whispered. "Before I go, there's something I need to know."

"What?" The word came so quietly, with such resolution, that she wondered if he knew what the question was.

"I need to know what really happened in Korea."

"I already told you."

"Not everything. Please, Marcus. Tell me everything."

He was silent for a long moment, staring at the ceiling as if the catastrophic event were unfolding in his mind. "I can't," he said.

"Please . . ."

His breathing came heavier, and he closed his eyes. When he opened them, they were filled with tears, and she knew that was rare in his life.

Downstairs, the clock on the wall cuckooed, and a chime played as the little Dutch girl danced around to mark the hour. Then all was quiet again, and the night settled around them like a warm blanket.

"It's a deadly secret," he whispered. "You'll see me differently."

"I love you," she said. "And no matter what you tell me, it won't change that."

He drew in a ragged sigh and covered his eyes with his hand. "There was an attack real close to our MASH unit, and we had dozens of incoming casualties. It was a horrible night, people screaming and crying, men dying, medics running here and there. . . . We were low on blood and antibiotics, so we were doing the best we could already. And then the shelling got closer. . . ."

He stopped and swallowed and forced himself to go on. "We had no choice but to bug out, so we loaded as many patients as we could into trucks, took as much medicine and supplies as we could get, and ran. But there were a few casualties who just couldn't be moved...at least, not the way we were having to do it. We were left with the choice of moving them anyway, knowing they'd die before we got where we were going, or just leaving them there. I couldn't stand either choice, so I kept a few supplies, and I stayed behind with them until they could come back for us."

He got quiet, and Sarah raised up on an elbow and looked at him. "How close was the shelling?"

"Real close," he said. "A village not more than five miles away had been hit, and I could see the flames up over the trees. And the noise...I've never heard noise like that in my life. The smell of smoke was almost smothering. I was dug into a hole with my patients, just waiting it out. But the funny thing was...as long as I could hear the noise, I had the feeling that everything would be all right. It wasn't until the noise stopped that I started to lose my mind, little by little."

"What happened?"

He moved his hand from his eyes, and she saw the ghosts there, the terror, the memories that would plague him until the day he died. "I sat in that foxhole, with my gun aimed, watching, waiting for any kind of movement, any threatening sound.... We had come through that nightmare, and I knew the trucks would be coming back for us again soon. So I kept watching...and waiting...."

Tears filled his eyes, ran down his temples.

"And then I heard something in the trees across the compound. A limb crack, or a branch rustle. I aimed at the sound, and waited—" His voice cracked, and he cleared his throat and went on. "One of the men in the hole with me moaned, and I knew that whoever was in those bushes knew we were there."

He covered his face again, and his body began to shake with the force of his misery. Sarah slipped her arms around his neck, cradled him and kissed the tears on his temple.

"I put my finger on the trigger and waited . . . and then . . . there was a deeper shadow in the brush, and someone started moving toward me, running. . . .

"God, Sarah, I opened fire, and I shot until I didn't have any bullets left. The person dropped, and I knew I had hit him. And there was silence again, so deep, so thick, and I sat hunched in that hole, watching for the rest of the night. Waiting . . .

"It wasn't until dawn that I was able to crawl out of that hole."

"Did you find him?" she asked softly.

"Yeah, I found him." His face twisted, and he squeezed his eyes shut. "I found the lifeless, bullet-filled body of a seven-year-old Korean boy who had fled from his burning village to look for help."

"Oh, my God." Her own tears spilled over her face, and finally Marcus met her eyes.

"That's why I'm being punished, Sarah. I'm destined to go on waiting . . . and waiting . . . and waiting . . . for you to get sicker and sicker each time you come back to me, until what? You die? Or for you to be born and grow into an adult that I can stalk until I die? Right now I'm lying here waiting for you to disappear... and then I'll wait for you to come back.... It's hell on earth, Sarah. Deeper than any I could imagine in the afterlife."

His arms closed around her, and she held him with every ounce of emotion she could summon within herself. Every fiber of her being. Every emotion in her soul.

This time, their lovemaking was slow, languorous, poignant enough to last two lifetimes, and Sarah tried with every touch and every kiss to convince him that she was more blessing than curse, and that he was not tainted by the guilt that still reigned in his soul.

But time caught up with them, and before she could try to heal the scars that festered within him, she heard Caren's voice calling from far away. "Oh, no," she whispered. "She's calling."

His embrace grew tighter, more desperate. Wiping away his tears, she kissed him one last time. "I love you, Marcus."

Sarah! Sarah!

"Oh, God, don't go!"

"I'll be back," she said, her own voice growing weaker as Caren's grew stronger. "I promise, Marcus. I'll be back."

CHAPTER TEN

Caren was halfway up the stairs when she heard the thud in the bedroom, and she broke into a run. "Sarah!"

She found her sister lying on the floor, pale as death and not moving, and she fell to her knees beside her. "Oh, God, Sarah!" She took her wrist and felt the slow, erratic heartbeat, as if it was on its last spurt before running out entirely. "No! Sarah!"

She reached for the telephone and dialed 911, and as she waited for the ambulance, she sat beside her sister, shaking her to wake her, as if the very movement would somehow stimulate her heart into reacting.

But Sarah didn't stir.

Again, as the ambulance arrived and they hooked her to IVs and monitors, Caren rode with her to the hospital. All the way there, she stared at her sister, knowing she was slipping away from her, knowing that she was losing her.

What was happening to her?

The thought of being without that vital other part of herself—her twin—was more than she could bear, and even though she knew that Sarah wasn't conscious to feel it, she took her hand and squeezed it. "Oh, Sarah, please don't leave me."

Tears rolled down her cheeks. She thought of Sarah as a child, a mirror image of herself. They had been best friends, soul sisters in the deepest sense of the word. Where they were different, their differences complemented each other.

She remembered Sarah's daydreaming as a child, how she had caught her one time in the attic of their grandmother's house, dressed in her mother's strapless prom dress, with her hair all teased and bound on her head. "You look silly," Caren had said, pulling out a set of shoulder pads their father had worn to play football. She'd set them on her shoulders, trying to top her sister's silliness, but when she'd looked up, ready for Sarah to stumble back, laughing at her, she'd seen a wistful look on her face as she gazed at her reflection in the mirror.

"Whatcha thinking about?" she'd asked.

"Just things," Sarah had said, locking away that part of herself.

Caren wondered now what kinds of things her sister had hidden from her then, and what she hid now. She had lied about Cancún. When Mick had called her, looking for Sarah, she'd realized it had all been an elaborately designed story. The odd thing was that she'd missed a shoot to do whatever she was doing, and it wasn't like Sarah to jeopardize her career. She never kept people waiting, never inconvenienced them in any way.

Had she been lying in that bedroom all this time, sick and dying and unable to reach the phone?

Something told Caren that she would have known. There had been other times in her life when Sarah had been sick, or a crisis had occurred, and she had felt it. The time Sarah had fallen off her bike and gotten a concussion, Caren had told her aunt immediately that something had happened. The time she had wrecked her car and had to have stitches for a cut in her leg, Caren had known.

Wouldn't she have known now if Sarah had been dying, trying to call her, waiting for help?

Maybe not, she thought. The bond between them was not infallible, by any means, and she supposed that her focus on Jimmy might be costing her a little of the bond she had with her sister. Maybe she would never have those feelings again.

Or maybe they still worked, and nothing had happened until just the moment when she'd found her.

Jimmy met the ambulance at the hospital, and Caren fell into his arms as they pulled Sarah out. "She's dying, Jimmy."

"No, she's not," he said, taking her hand and pulling her into the emergency room behind the gurney. "She's going to be okay."

"We don't know that." She tried to follow through the door, but a nurse stopped her and told her to stay in the waiting room until the doctor came out. She sat stiffly, sickly, waiting as the moments ticked by, as her sister lay in that room fighting for her life. She had never felt so helpless.

When the doctor came out, he looked frustrated, tired and confused.

"Is she all right, doctor?"

"We've stabilized her," he said. "Her heartbeat is a little more stable, and she's breathing better. Her fever is dangerously high, though, and until we can get it stabilized, we're moving her to intensive care." He took off his glasses, rubbed his eyes and focused on Caren. "Has she undergone any kind of physical trauma lately?"

"Nothing that I know of," Caren said. "There have been some emotional things...."

"No," he said. "Whatever this is, it isn't subtle. Something has happened to her to wreak havoc on her system. I can't imagine what. Radiation exposure, maybe, or a poison we're not picking up in the blood tests...."

"Oh, my God," Caren whispered, coming to her feet. Jimmy pulled her against him, sheltering her from the pain, and she clung to him until she was able to look at the doctor again. "Just tell me, Doctor, is she going to make it?"

"It's touch and go right now," he said. "We're doing the best we can."

The words were as much a pronouncement of death as any Caren had ever heard, and she broke down and buried her face against her husband's shirt. He held her, whispering hope into her ear, comforting her with what little comfort he could offer.

Finally a nurse came for her and told her she could see Sarah. Wiping her eyes, she went to her sister.

The color had returned to her sister's face, and her breathing seemed more normal, but when Caren bent over to touch her, she jumped at the heat radiating from her forehead. What if the fever caused brain damage, or killed her altogether? And why hadn't they been able to get it down?

She crumpled into tears once again and, looking her sister in the face, said, "Don't you leave me, Sarah. I'll never forgive you if you do."

There was no answer, only the sound of Sarah's heart beating on the monitor. But Caren stayed by her side, anyway, watching and waiting, until morning intruded in the room and she fell asleep in the chair beside the bed.

Sarah woke and saw her sister asleep in the chair next to her bed, and before she could process where she was or how she'd gotten there, she was walloped by a fierce throbbing in her head and a raging nausea in her stomach.

She grabbed for the bedpan next to her and heaved into it, waking Caren instantly. Her sister sprang to her side, holding back her hair, taking the bedpan, muttering that it would be all right.

When Sarah fell back onto her pillow, an overwhelming weakness weighed her down. "How long have I been like this?" she asked.

"I don't know," Caren said. "I found you about fifteen hours ago, but I don't know how long you were sick before I found you."

Sarah closed her eyes and tried to will away the nausea and the throbbing in her head. "That's longer than last time. And it feels like I'm only halfway through it."

Caren shot her a strange look. "Sarah, do you know what's wrong with you?"

"What are the doctors saying?"

"Some of them think it's another virus, but a few are trying to examine the possibility that you've been poisoned in some way, or that you've been exposed to some type of radiation. Have you, Sarah? Is there anything you can think of that would have gotten you like this?"

Sarah opened her eyes and tried to focus on the ceiling, wondering whether to tell her sister everything. Would she believe that she had traveled through time? *Could* she believe it? She glanced at her sister, saw the worry etching itself on her features and told herself that it wasn't something anyone could accept lightly.

"No," she whispered. "Nothing."

Caren took her hand and leaned forward, meeting her sister's eyes directly. "Is there any new film you've been working with, new chemicals, new machinery? Anything that might be causing you to have an adverse reaction?"

"No," Sarah said.

Caren was quiet for a moment, and then her mouth began to tremble. "Sarah, why are you lying to me?"

Sarah's gaze snapped to Caren. "What do you mean?"

"I'm your sister," she said. "I know when you're keeping something from me. What is it?"

Sarah felt cornered, but she still couldn't tell the truth. "When I was in the Bahamas, one of the models got sick. She had these same symptoms and—"

"You said Cancún," Caren bit out. "And you were never there. Mick was looking for you."

Sarah's mouth went dry, and she closed her eyes and tried not to give in to the smothering sense of fatigue and the still-roiling nausea in her stomach. "All right, so I lied."

"Where were you, Sarah?"

"At home," she said truthfully. "I was . . . working on a project, and I needed absolute silence and no interruptions."

"Did it have anything to do with that old camera that was set up on your tripod?"

Sarah sent her a guilty look that spoke volumes. "No," she said, too quickly.

Caren's face reddened, and her lips compressed. "Sarah, you're lying to me again. What does that camera have to do with this?"

Sarah made a concerted effort to relax and try not to be so defensive. "Nothing, Caren. You're just starting to get on my nerves. I'm lying here trying to decide whether to throw up or try to make it to the bathroom, my head is throbbing and I'm freezing to death, and you're giving me the third degree about some old camera in my darkroom."

Caren softened instantly. "I'm sorry. Really, I didn't mean to be like that." She got up and pulled the blanket up. "You're having chills. Your fever's still real high. Let me call the nurse."

She left the room for a moment, and Sarah closed her eyes and told herself that she'd gotten off the hook this time. But it had been close.

She couldn't let Caren link the camera to her illness, or she might try to take matters into her own hands. As for the time travel and Marcus, it was something her sister would never be able to understand as long as she lived.

It was her secret, hers to bear alone, and hers to work out the best way she could. For the moment, her main goal was getting her strength back so that she could figure out how to get back to Marcus once and for all.

Her fever raged for two more days, and her stomach rejected everything that reached it, and Sarah couldn't fight the impatience she felt toward her illness. It was keeping her from getting back to Marcus. What was he thinking? Was he grieving? And did he believe that she'd ever come back?

She heard a knock on the door of her hospital room, and Mick stuck his head in. "Okay to come in?" he asked.

She smiled. "Hi, Mick. Sure, come on in."

"I hear you're feeling pretty rough," he said. "How do you feel now?"

"Better," she said. "As long as they feed me through the IV, I guess I'll live."

"So when are they gonna spring you?"

"Whenever I feel I can get up and walk out of here. But don't worry. I'm sure I'll be well in time for the Elizabeth Arden shoot. I don't—"

"You missed it already," he said quietly. "We had to get Pete Johnson to shoot it."

"Oh." She frowned, struggling to remember what day it was. "I'm sorry. I get confused about the time."

"That's understandable. I've postponed the shoots that I can, until you get better, and the others I've reassigned. You don't need to put any pressure on yourself, Sarah. You've been really sick."

"But it'll go away before I know it," she assured him. "Last time it did."

"You're sicker than you were last time."

"It just means it takes longer to recover, but once I get through this I'll be fine."

"I'd just feel better not scheduling anything for a while," he said, with a soft note of finality. He cocked a grin and leaned forward. "I'm trying to think of some test or something to put you through to decide when you're well enough to work."

"A test? What kind?"

He shrugged, as if he hadn't given it much thought. "Something...sexual, perhaps. Just to test your stamina, of course."

She grinned. "For my own good, right?"

"Right. After all, what's in it for me?"

"Nice try," she said. "And you know, that might even work on one of the younger models. Have you tried it?"

"It works on everybody but you," he said. "Personally, I think you're frigid."

Her smile faded, and she shook her head. "No, I'm definitely not that."

"Then there must be somebody else."

She laughed. "Maybe."

"I knew it," he said, slapping his knee. "Somebody beat me to you. Damn it, when do I get to meet him? You've got to let me check out the competition."

Her smile faded completely. "I don't know," she said. "He's . . . he's from out of town."

"Terrific. Well, if you get lonely sometime, give me a call. I'm not the jealous type." He got up and pressed a kiss to her forehead, then started for the door.

Before he left, he threw a wink at her over his shoulder. Sarah laughed as he closed the door behind him.

Caren made her way through the maze of offices in Mick's ad agency and saw him through a glass wall, dunking baskets in a hoop above the door. She watched while he made a slam dunk, then raised his arms victoriously and strutted back to his desk.

Tentatively she knocked. "Mick?"

He swung around, still breathing hard, and a smile came instantly to his face. "Caren! What're you doing here?"

She came into his office. "Can I close the door? I need to talk to you."

"Sure," he said, perching on the edge of his desk and crossing his arms. "What's up? Is Sarah all right?"

"She seems better," she said. "It's weird." She shook her head and gave him a long, serious look. "Mick, Sarah told me you visited her yesterday. Did she tell you anything?"

"Anything like what?"

"I don't know," Caren said. "Anything about a project she's working on, or where she had been for the last few days, before I found her?"

He grinned and tossed the ball at the hoop again. It rolled around the rim and bounced out to the floor. "No, we didn't really talk about it. I figure she was just with her boyfriend. I guess she's entitled, although I wish she had let me know so I could rearrange her schedule."

"Boyfriend?" Caren tried to erase the hurt look from her eyes and schooled her face to look unaffected. "What boyfriend is that?"

"Whoever it is that's got her all moony eyed. She said he lived out of town."

Irritation tormented her face even more. "Out of town where?"

"Got me. She didn't say much more about him."

"Not a name or anything?" Now the frustration on her face showed through in living color, and Mick stood up straight and gave her a concerned look.

"Sorry, Caren. She hasn't told you about him?"

"No, she hasn't." She looked down at the floor, her brain running through possible reasons Sarah would have to keep it to herself. But, despite her efforts, she couldn't think of one. Sarah had always told her everything, even the things she was ashamed of.

"Well, maybe she thought you'd just know. Aren't twins supposed to be psychic or something?"

Caren forced a weak smile. "Not like that." She sighed and started back toward the door. "Thanks, Mick. I appreciate your help."

"So... is she gonna be all right?"

"Yeah, I think so," she said. "We've just got to figure out what keeps making her so sick. By the way, you haven't put her to work near any toxic-waste dumps, have you?"

He looked thoughtful for a moment. "Well, there was that *Sports Illustrated* bathing-suit edition we did on that plutonium dump last week. Nah, that couldn't be it."

Caren grinned at his impishness. "Seriously, Mick. Has she mentioned using any new film or equipment, or is she using something different to process it?"

He shrugged. "The only thing different I've noticed is that old camera she found in her attic. It made some interesting-looking pictures of the Sweeter-Than-Sin-Yogurt people."

"Her attic?" Something strange, the beginning of fear, spiraled up in her bloodstream. "She found it in her attic, and she's been using it?"

"Well, some. She's probably lost interest in it by now, but she couldn't wait to use it at the party."

"I see." Frowning, she opened the door. "It's probably nothing. Well, I'll see you later."

"Yeah. I'll come up and check on her again in a day or two."

Caren nodded and left him in his office. As she made her way back out to her car, she couldn't escape the ragged feeling that the old camera had something to do with Sarah's obsession with Marcus. But Sarah hadn't mentioned him lately. And that in itself was strange.

Instead of going back to the hospital, she went to Sarah's house, walked in with the key her sister had given her and headed for the darkroom. That camera was still set up on the tripod.

Quickly she unhooked it, set it in a paper sack and drove to the hospital, trying hard to fight the sinking feeling that Sarah was in grave danger, but that Caren would have to figure out just what it was—and how this camera tied in—all by herself.

Sarah sat back against her pillows, a tray of empty dishes on her lap. It was the first meal she'd been able to keep down, and even though it was only soup and Jell-O, she supposed she was making progress. The fact that this illness had hung on so long frightened her. It was getting worse each time, and she feared that many more trips might do her in. But she couldn't risk not going back to Marcus.

She heard a soft knock on the door and looked up to see her sister coming in. Caren had one of those looks on her face, the kind that said she was worried and irritated with her sister, and Sarah didn't know what she'd done. "What's wrong?" she asked.

"Why do you think something's wrong?"

"Oh, the look on your face, for one thing."

Caren tried to smile. "No, I'm fine. How are you?"

"I ate," she said, looking down at the empty dishes. Holding up her arm, she said, "Look, sis, no IV."

"That's great," Caren said, and her color brightened just a little. "What has the doctor said?"

"That I might be going home in a few days." She set her tray on the table beside her bed. "But I told him that I'd stay until tomorrow at the very latest."

"Sarah." The stern voice reminded Sarah of their aunt, and she smiled at her sister.

"Well, why should I hang around in here doing nothing when I've got important things I could be doing instead?"

"Important things like what?" That look was back, and Sarah felt as if she'd been caught at something. She just wasn't sure what.

"Work, for one thing. Mick didn't reschedule everything, you know."

"Mick doesn't know which end is up with you, Sarah. He isn't counting on anything. Nobody is."

Sarah's humor vanished, and she looked hard at her sister. "Caren, tell me what's wrong."

The tears that burst into Caren's eyes surprised her, and she started to get out of the bed. "What's wrong?"

"You've been lying to me, Sarah, and I don't know why." Her face reddened, and Sarah saw Caren reverting to that little girl who had always seemed to get her feelings hurt.

"About what? What do you think I've lied about?"

"Your boyfriend, for one thing. Why didn't you tell me about him?"

Mick, Sarah thought. He'd told her, and now she'd have to come up with some explanation that made sense. "Caren, there's no boyfriend. If you heard that from Mick, I only told him that so he'd quit begging for me to go out with him."

Caren shook her head. "No, that's not true. I can tell there's something you're keeping from me. And God knows, if you want to keep it a secret for some reason, you're entitled. I have no right to be hurt, and that's not the point, really." She stopped and grabbed a tissue, blew her nose. "The main thing is that I want to find out what keeps making you so sick, but you don't seem the slightest bit concerned about helping me."

"It's a virus," Sarah said. "All the doctors said so."

"Then why is this the second time you've gotten it? If it's a virus, how come you got over it once and it came back?"

Sarah shook her head, confused. "What do *you* think it is, Caren?"

Caren came closer, her eyes still thick with tears. "I think you've been exposed to some kind of physical trauma." She reached for her bag, dug into it. "Sarah, I want you to think, really hard. Were you playing with this when you got sick?"

Sarah watched as Caren pulled the camera out of her bag, and suddenly she felt the room spinning, her world tilting, and her only chance of getting back to Marcus slipping away. "No," she said, too loudly. Then she slipped her feet to the ground and lurched for the camera.

Surprised at Sarah's desperation to get it back, Caren stumbled back. "Sarah!"

"Give it to me, Caren. It's a priceless antique, and I don't want anything to happen to it."

She was sweating, she realized, and her heart was pounding, and those damn monitors hooked to her kept her from getting any closer to her sister.

Caren only gaped at her. "Just answer me, Sarah. Were you using this when you got sick?"

"No!" Sarah shouted. "It has nothing to do with this."

"Mick said you found it in the attic. Does this have something to do with that Stephen Marcus fellow?"

Sarah's breathing grew thicker, and suddenly it was impossible to get enough air into her lungs. "His name is Marcus Stephens, and, no, it has nothing to do with him. Caren, you're overstepping your bounds now. Please . . . just give me back the camera."

The door burst open, and one of the nurses dashed in. "Your monitor set off an alarm," she said, forcing Sarah back to the bed. She checked her pulse, then quickly paged the doctor.

All the while, Sarah kept her eyes on that camera, and as she reached toward Caren, beseeching her to give it back, her hands trembled.

"What happened?" the nurse asked.

Caren shook her head. "I don't know. I upset her, I'm afraid. Is she all right?"

The nurse didn't answer, for she was too busy checking Sarah's blood pressure and sticking a thermometer in her mouth. After a moment, the doctor burst in and examined her.

It didn't faze her that people were poking and prodding all over her, for her only thought was the camera that Caren held in her hands.

Tears came to her eyes, and she whispered, "Caren, please . . ."

The doctor gave her a shot, and she jolted with the pain, and suddenly a sweet sleepiness washed over her. Confusion clouded her brain, and she felt herself slipping into sleep, but something kept holding her back. "Caren, I need the camera," she whispered in a small, distant voice. "Please . . . I've got to get back to him. . . ."

Sleep overcame her before Caren gave the camera back.

CHAPTER ELEVEN

Marcus hadn't been in St. Theresa's Catholic Hospital since before he'd left for Korea, but as he entered the lobby now, he realized that nothing had changed. The antiseptic smell he'd grown used to still wafted in the air, and people still spoke with low voices while nurses walked rapidly through the halls.

He found Gene's office and knocked lightly, not expecting anyone to answer. Gene was probably in surgery right about now, and he could simply leave the supplies he'd borrowed beside his desk.

But behind the door, he heard Gene call, "Come in."

Marcus opened the door and smiled at his old friend. "Hey, buddy."

"Mark!" Gene sprang from his chair and came around the desk to shake his friend's hand. "I don't believe you actually showed your face in daylight. I thought you'd given up sunshine."

Marcus's smile faded. "Not quite."

He noticed the bag in Marcus's hand, and took it. "You brought the stuff back, huh? I've been meaning to get over to pick it up. How's the patient?"

"Fine," he said. "Fully recovered." Even as he said the words, though, he realized that she'd had that illness waiting for her again on the other side. A sick feeling rose inside him, and he uttered a silent prayer that she'd pulled through all right.

What if she didn't?

Gene set the bag on his desk. "Why didn't you bring her to the hospital?"

"Her?" Marcus asked. "What makes you think it was a her?"

Gene grinned as if he'd been holding a secret tight and couldn't wait to get rid of it. "I heard. You were seen in town last Saturday night with some little brunette beauty."

He rolled his eyes. "We didn't even go in anywhere."

"Sorita Simpson claims to have seen you in the drugstore."

"Oh, yeah," he said. "I did go there. What else did she say?"

"That this little lady had drawn out the first smile anyone had seen from you since you got back from the war."

Marcus couldn't find that smile in him now. "Yeah, I guess she did."

"So when do I get to meet her?"

"Never."

His friend gave him a questioning look, and Marcus started back to the door. Somehow he just couldn't talk about it. She was gone, she might never be back, and if she did come back, she couldn't stay. It was an altogether impossible situation.

"Why not?" Gene asked. "You ashamed of your old pal?"

"Of course not," he said. "She's just... We're not... you know... I may never see her again myself."

"Then it wasn't serious?"

Even knowing how easy that answer would be, Marcus couldn't make himself say it. "It's not meant to be," he said. "A lot of things are just not meant to be."

He could see the concern on Gene's face. Unable to appease it, he went back to the door. "Thanks for the help, man. I don't know what I would have done without you."

Then he left Gene standing in his office, watching him as if he didn't know what to think.

Sarah awoke groggy the next day, and the moment she realized where she was and that she had been sedated, a fury greater than any she had ever known raged through her. Sitting up, she saw her sister in a chair, reading a newspaper.

"Caren, how long have I been out?"

"Ten hours or so," she said. "You were pretty upset. They gave you something to calm you down."

"They gave me something to knock me out." She got out of bed, staggering toward the closet. Caren sprang out of her chair and tried to help, but Sarah shoved her away. "I'm getting out of here."

"Sarah, that's insane! You're in no shape to check out!"

Sarah spun around and grasped onto the closet door. "Where's the camera, Caren? What did you do with it?"

Caren couldn't believe her ears. "I took it home," she said. "I was worried it was causing the problem, but—"

"Then take me to get it," Sarah cut in, reaching for the clothes Caren had left for her in the closet. "Now."

"Sarah! I can't! You haven't been released yet!"

"I'm releasing myself." She pulled her gown over her head and slipped into her blouse. "You didn't do anything to it, did you?"

"To what?"

"The camera, damn it! You didn't break it or take it apart or anything, did you?"

"No, of course not!"

"Thank God." She slipped into her skirt, then found her shoes against the wall. "Come on, Caren. Take me to your house."

Caren stood looking at her in disbelief. "What has gotten into you? What's so important about a stupid camera?"

Sarah's hand trembled as she brought it to her forehead. "I told you, it's an antique."

"So you'd get up from a drugged sleep and wobble like a drunk out of here just to protect an antique that I've already told you is safe?"

"I don't like people messing with my things."

"Since when?" Caren returned. "I've always messed with your things."

"Then it's time you stopped!" She grabbed the rest of her things, slung them into her suitcase, zipped it up. "Let's go."

"But the nurse— You have to tell somebody, Sarah."

"They'll figure it out eventually," she said. She was starting toward the door, dragging the suitcase with her, when she felt a wave of dizziness and clutched at the wall. Caren caught her before she fainted.

"You're not going anywhere until the doctors release you," she said, making her sit down.

"Then get them to bring the forms in here," she said. "I'm leaving this hospital, Caren, whether you help me or not."

Throwing up her hands, Caren rushed out into the hall, and Sarah dropped her face into her hands, wondering if the illness she still felt had more to do with the trauma or the drug. Her sickness had never held on this long before. It seemed like she'd never get well.

Two nurses came back with Caren, insisting that Sarah stay in bed, but when she finally convinced them that she was leaving, with or without their blessing, they gathered the necessary forms and let her leave.

Caren didn't speak to her all the way home, and Sarah's mind was too focused on that camera to think of any idle chitchat. The moment they reached Caren's driveway, Sarah opened the door. "Where's the camera?"

"Good grief, Sarah—it's in the study. What is the big hurry?"

Sarah tried to stay calm as Caren got her purse and led her to the front door. Jimmy greeted them at the door.

"Sarah! Caren didn't tell me you were getting out today."

Sarah didn't respond. Instead, she just pushed past him into the study and looked around. She heard Caren whisper something behind her, and just as Sarah was about to scream out that she didn't see the camera anywhere, Caren reached up to an upper bookshelf and got it down.

"Here's your camera," she said, thrusting it at her sister.

Sarah's relief as she examined the camera and discovered that it had been untouched was profound. There was no reason why it wouldn't still work . . . but that didn't satisfy her entirely, for there was really no reason why it should have worked in the first place. What if it had to do with sitting in the same house all these years? What if moving it had broken the spell?

Clutching it like a newborn baby, she fluttered down onto the sofa. "Thank you," she whispered. "It looks all right."

Bursting into tears, Caren sat down next to her. "Sarah, please level with me. What's going on?"

Sarah dropped her head back on the sofa. "There are things . . . that you'd never understand. Not in a million years."

"He's married, isn't he?"

Sarah's eyes came open. "Who?"

"The guy you're in love with. Either that, or he's of some other race. Those are the only two things I can figure out. Which is it?"

"Neither," Sarah said wearily. "It's nothing like that." Tears came to her own eyes, and she wiped them away. She looked over at her sister, realized how upset she had made her, and suddenly a deep remorse filled her heart. Caren didn't understand, but that wasn't her fault. And Sarah had no right to hurt her the way she had.

"I'm sorry for the way I acted, sis. I love you."

"I love you," Caren returned. "But somehow I feel like I'm losing you. And the worst part is, I don't know to what—or to whom."

Sarah took her hand, squeezed it and considered for a long moment telling her the whole story. But Caren would only think she had snapped, and if she did by some remote chance believe her, she'd try to keep her from going back to Marcus. No, she couldn't tell her everything. But she could tell her enough to calm her a little.

"Caren, you know when we were kids, and we'd go to birthday parties and stuff, and I never really felt like I fit in?"

"You're still that way a little," Caren said.

"Yeah, I am. Like I've never felt comfortable where I am." She looked wistfully across the room, staring at nothing. "And all the men I've dated, they've been wrong for me somehow. They're not like the man I dream of, nothing like him. Sometimes I feel like I was put into the wrong time by accident. Like I would have fared so much better in an earlier time, when things were simpler and I could be simpler."

She could see that Caren was struggling to see what this had to do with anything, but she knew she couldn't be more specific.

"But...you aren't unhappy, are you?" Caren asked. "Your life is so full, you have your work, your friends, me...."

"But nothing of my own," she said quietly. "Caren, as long as I've lived, I've never had anything of my own."

"Hey, that's the hazard of being a twin," Caren whispered.

"Not really. You have Jimmy, don't you?"

"And you'll have someone soon," Caren assured her. "Just be patient. When you find him, you'll know, and everything will fall into place."

"Unless everything had to be out of place for me to find him in the first place."

Caren's face distorted. "What are you saying?"

Sarah wiped her tears away and focused on her sister, more seriously, more intently, than she'd ever done before. "Caren, if I were to disappear without a trace and never come back, would you try to think of me as happier? Finally in a place where I belong and where I have something of my own?"

Caren's face twisted and more tears fell. "Where are you going, Sarah?" she whispered.

Sarah squeezed her hand tighter. For a moment she thought of saying, *Back to Marcus, because I love him fiercely, Caren, and I truly don't think I can live without him.* But, instead, she shook her head and said, "Nowhere. I don't know. I'm just saying, if I did go away, you shouldn't grieve. You have Jimmy now, and you can be happy without me."

"I'll always need you, Sarah. You're a part of me."

"And I feel the same way. But what we've been to each other, what we are, can't ever be taken from us. Just because we're not together doesn't mean we don't mean anything to each other. Sometimes sacrifices just have to be made. Choices. Hard ones."

Caren only cried harder, and finally she whispered, "I wish I knew what you were talking about. Why can't I read your mind when I need to?"

Sarah pulled her into her arms and held her while her sister cried her heart out.

Later that night, it was Jimmy who held Caren and let her cry. After an hour, she looked up at him, her face wet, and whispered, "I think she's going to die."

"Why?"

"I think she knows something about her illness that she isn't telling me. Maybe she knows she has something that's killing her, and she doesn't want me to worry. Why else would she warn me not to grieve?"

"I don't know," Jimmy whispered against her hair. "But where does the camera fit in?"

"God, I wish I knew," Caren said. "Jimmy, if anything ever happens to her, I just don't know what I'll do."

"Shh," he said, holding her tighter. "Nothing's going to happen. Sarah's going to be just fine."

Downstairs, in the guest room, Sarah lay staring at the ceiling, wishing for someone to hold her and convince her that things would work out in this madness her life had become.

From the depths of her soul, she missed Marcus.

What was he doing now? she wondered. Had he given up on her? And what if moving the camera from the house had changed its properties somehow? What if she couldn't get back to him again?

And why did she still feel so weak?

Tears rolled down her temples as she tried to sleep, and when she finally did, it was from sheer exhaustion. But even as she slept, her mind continued to seek Marcus.

Marcus couldn't sleep, so he got up and dressed and stepped outside into the darkness. He began to walk, letting the fall breeze whisper around him, ruffling his disheveled hair. He walked outside of his neighborhood, turned up the main road and passed the little church where his relatives were buried. She had wanted to go in there, but there hadn't been time. Now he wondered if she'd ever get the chance.

He walked farther, up toward the bridge that she'd said hadn't changed in forty-some years. She had stood on it, looking out, and thought how similar that one view looked to her time. When he reached it, he walked out over it, leaned on the rail in the same place where they had stood together and tried to imagine her in the same place...on the other side of that curtain that separated their times.

The water rippled below him, and he gazed down, thinking how inviting it had seemed at different times in his life. When he was a boy, he had swum upriver a ways, but his parents had warned him never to swim out toward the bridge, for the undercurrent was too strong. Despite his curiosity, his few attempts to buck their advice had convinced him they were right.

He remembered camping out there when he was in college, he and Gene and some of the others he'd lost touch with over the years. They'd roasted hot dogs over an open fire, told ghost stories and swatted mosquitoes, then gone for midnight swims.

So long ago.

And then, not that long ago, when the memories of the war had pushed him beyond the limits of endurance, he had stood on this same bridge and looked at the river as a refuge. An escape. A way to end the pain.

But Sarah had changed all that, and now he saw the river as a link to her, something she saw every day wherever she was, something that meant beauty and goodness to her. The mere possibility of her coming back kept him from thinking of the river in those ugly, suicidal terms anymore. If he could live to see her even one more time, he would wait as long as it took.

Slowly he left the bridge and headed back home, hoping beyond hope that she'd be there waiting for him when he got back. But somewhere deep in his gut he knew his hope was in vain.

CHAPTER TWELVE

Sarah tried jogging to get into shape, but after only a few yards she was so out of breath that she had to slow to a walk. Her shorts hung on her hips, at least a size too big, but her big shirt concealed the ribs that were starting to show through her skin.

She wasn't getting her strength back, the way she was supposed to. She was tired all the time and had trouble keeping all her food down, so she ate tiny portions frequently during the day. She felt like someone suffering from some debilitating disease, and vaguely, as she tried to finish her walk, she wondered if she had in fact developed one after all the trauma she'd put her body through.

She wiped a tear away and told herself that it could take months to restore her body, months of miserable waiting and wondering if the camera would still send her back.

Too tired to go on, she stopped at the top of the bridge and decided to go back. Her heart was beating too fast, and she felt dizzy, so she sat down and dropped her face in her arms. She could do this for the rest of her life, she thought. Go back to him, get sicker, wait for Caren to call her back, get sicker still, then spend months recuperating before she did it all again. It was the only way to keep seeing Marcus. But all the misery and suffering it would cause her in between almost made it seem impossible.

Unless she could find a way to say goodbye to her life here and stay with him.

But that, in itself, was impossible, for Caren would always be there to call her back. And as much as she wanted to be with him, she couldn't yet bear the thought of never seeing her sister again.

Her heart slowed to a more normal pace, and her breathing settled, so she got up and walked, more slowly, back down the hill. She passed the old church, which was rotting and boarded up, and went behind it to the graveyard, which had grown over with weeds. Marcus had people here, she thought. His parents, aunts and uncles, grandparents....

She tore the weeds off one of the headstones and read the name. Claudia Stephens Boyd—1890-1949. She smiled and touched the granite, wondering if Claudia had been an aunt of Marcus's. Next to her was William Boyd, her husband, and the headstone read 1888-1955. Marcus hadn't seen him buried yet.

Strolling through, she found other headstones with names she didn't recognize, then stumbled on another Stephens couple. Marcus Stephens, Sr., the headstone read. 1895-1950. Could that be his father?

Then, almost frantically, she tore the vines off the headstone next to it, wiped the caked dirt off the inscription: Amanda Stephens, 1898-1947. Five years before she'd met Marcus.

He should be buried here with his family, she thought, leaning back against the headstone and wondering why no one had put him here, why they hadn't known, why he'd just been a lonely old man with only a handful of people at his grave site. Why had he been buried in a pine box in a nondescript cemetery that meant nothing to him when he could have been laid here with his parents and his family?

I'll have him moved, she thought, cutting across the overgrown yard and heading home. I'll clean the graveyard up, plant flowers on all the graves, and move Marcus's body here where he belongs.

She turned the corner to her street, and suddenly the reality assailed her: He was dead and gone, and it didn't really matter where he was buried, because his life had been wasted. He had spent it looking for her, waiting out a torture in the cruelest of hells. And she would spend hers waiting, too.

She picked up speed and found herself jogging again, out of determination more than stamina, as she neared her house. She had to get back to him, she told herself. She had to see him again and make sure that, if she couldn't figure out a way to stay with him, he wouldn't waste his life again, that he wouldn't give up everything he loved, that he would become something more than a sad man who had no one but his land-lady to care for him.

Marcus had to change his destiny, and it was up to her to help him.

She ran in the door, her heart hammering and her breath coming almost in gasps, and she stumbled to her darkroom to find the camera. She would go back to him now, and if her body couldn't handle the trauma, he would save her. She knew he could.

She felt dizzy and almost fainted, and she forced herself to sit down. She set the camera in her lap, stared down at it and let her warm tears wash down over her face. She couldn't go back to him, not yet. Not until she was sure the trip wouldn't kill her. Not until her heart was stronger and her lungs were healthier. Being dizzy before she even made the trip was not a good sign.

But, damn it, she hoped she'd hurry and get well, because she feared she wouldn't be able to think straight until that day came.

Caren saw Sarah's car parked at the old abandoned church house before she'd made her way across the bridge, and, frowning, she pulled in beside her. Getting out, she looked around, but didn't see her sister. "Sarah?" she called.

From behind the old building, she heard her sister's voice. "Back here, Caren!"

She rounded the building, to the cemetery she hadn't even known was there, and saw Sarah knee-deep in weeds, gloves on her hands and a pile of debris beside her. Her face was smeared with dirt, and her face glistened with perspiration.

"What are you doing?"

"Cleaning out this place," Sarah said, pulling up the weeds almost frantically. "It's disgraceful, all these people buried here and forgotten. Someone should have taken care of the graves, but everything's all overgrown."

Caren stood gaping at her, astounded. It was one more inconsistency in Sarah's life, one more idiosyncrasy where there had never been any before, one more instance of inexplicable behavior. "Sarah, you hate gardening."

"I'm not gardening," Sarah said. "I'm cleaning." She got to her feet, wiped her hair back with one glove. "Look how sweet this place is, Caren. All these people who lived so long ago. Most of them were born in the nineteenth century. How could they have been forgotten?"

Caren only stared at her. "I don't know, Sarah." She thought of saying something about how they were dead and gone, and how it didn't really matter what their graves looked like, but somehow she didn't think that would go over too well. "Mick is looking for you. He's been trying to call, but you weren't answering the phone."

"That's because I'm not home," Sarah said with a smile.

Caren nodded. "Yeah, well, I was afraid you'd had another episode. That you were lying on the floor passed out or something. Never expected to find you here."

"What did he want?"

"To see when he could get you back to work, I guess."

"Oh." She dropped back to her knees and resumed pulling the weeds. "I don't think I'm ready yet. I haven't got my strength all the way back."

"Then you shouldn't be out here doing this," Caren said. "Sarah, what's the matter with you? When we were kids and Uncle Will would make us go in the backyard to rake or pull weeds, you were the one who would bribe me with your whole allowance to get me to do your work for you."

Sarah smiled. "You're right. Why don't you help me? You're the one with all the experience."

"It doesn't make sense," Caren said, not making a move to join in.

"Well, it doesn't have to make sense. It just is."

She watched as Sarah tore up some vines, uncovering a headstone, and ran her hand gently along the name engraved in it. Caren stepped forward and glanced at it, and saw the name Stephens.

She caught her breath and looked over at one of the other granite stones. "Marcus Stephens, Sr. Amanda Stephens." She spun back to her sister. "Sarah, what's going on?"

Sarah tore off some more vines and piled them next to her. "They're his parents, I think," she said. "I didn't even realize he was a Junior, but it makes sense."

Sarah looked up and saw the horrified look on Caren's face. "What?"

"I thought this obsession was over," Caren said. "I thought you'd gotten over it."

"I am over it," Sarah said. "It's not an obsession. I just stumbled on all this, and I realized they were his people. He should be buried here, don't you think? But no one knew. I'm thinking of trying to have him moved."

"His body?" Caren asked, stunned. "You've got to be kidding."

"Why?" Sarah asked. "Doesn't a person deserve to be buried with his family?"

She looked back at her sister and saw that Caren was crying. "What's wrong, Caren?"

Caren dropped to her knees beside her sister and put her arms around her. She pulled her into a strong embrace, and Sarah hugged her back. She felt Caren's body racking against her, heard the muffled sobs against her shoulder.

Why was Caren crying? She pulled back and looked her sister in the face, and she realized that something was tormenting her. Something terrible.

And then it struck her what it was.

"You think I'm crazy, don't you?"

Caren's mouth twisted, and her breath caught on a sob. "Sarah, this is...insane. Everything you've done lately. Your telling me you were going to Cancún when you were home all along, your reaction to the camera, and now this—" Her voice broke, and she looked around at the gravestones covered with vines and weeds. "I'm worried about you, Sarah."

She touched Sarah's face, framed it with her hands. "You need to be under a doctor's care, honey. Do you hear me? You need help, and I don't know how to give it to you."

"I don't need help," Sarah said, pulling back. "Caren, I'm not crazy. I swear I'm not."

"Maybe it doesn't seem that way to you," Caren whispered. "But you had a real high fever. What if...what if you have some brain damage from that? Nothing serious, but just something little that can still be fixed? An infection or something...."

"I don't have brain damage!" she said. "Caren, I'm fine."

"Then why are you acting like this, for God's sake? And why have you lost so much weight, and why are you keeping so many secrets?"

Sarah sat down again and looked off into the distance. "Just because I think a man ought to be buried with people he loved, you think I've snapped?"

"Just because it's so important to you!" Caren cried. "Maybe it's the medication they have you on or—I don't know, Sarah. But you have to see a doctor."

"All right," she said, giving in to appease Caren. "I'll make an appointment this afternoon."

"No, I'll make the appointment, and I'll take you there myself this afternoon," Caren said. "I want you to come with me right now, get cleaned up, and let me do that."

"No! I'm busy with this," she said. "There's a lot to do, Caren. So many graves to clean up. Somebody has to do this, and I've decided it's going to be me."

"Oh, God," Caren said, covering her mouth and sobbing again. She dropped her hands and nodded, as if reluctantly accepting what Sarah had said. "Then I guess I'll have to take matters into my own hands."

She started back to the car, and Sarah got to her feet. "What are you going to do, Caren?"

"Whatever it takes," she said.

"What does that mean?"

Caren didn't answer. Instead, she got into her car, looked back over her shoulder and pulled back out into the street before Sarah could stop her.

* * *

By the time Sarah ran out of energy and drove back home, she was almost certain that she knew what Caren was going to do. It was what Sarah would have done in the same situation. She would have done whatever she thought was in her sister's best interest. She would have used some sort of intervention to have her committed to a hospital.

Was she that certain Sarah was crazy?

She tried to think how Caren would do it. Would she try to trick her into walking into a hospital of her own volition, even though Sarah had shown such stubbornness lately? Or would she have them come and take her forcefully, like a fugitive, in handcuffs?

The thought sent a wave of rage through her, but then a part of her quelled that rage, telling her that she hadn't left Caren with a lot of choices.

She just didn't understand. Maybe the thing to do was to talk to her more. Tell her just enough to make her leave her alone.

But telling her that she'd traveled through time—not once, but twice—that she'd fallen in love with a man who was dead and buried, that she wanted more than anything to get back to him when she was strong enough, would only serve to reinforce Caren's belief that her sister had gone insane.

It was hopeless, she thought. She'd just have to let Caren think she was crazy and try to prove her wrong. But what if her sister had already set things in motion? What if she forced Sarah from her house, from the camera, and had her held in some hospital until they evaluated her condition?

She couldn't risk it, she thought. Even if she took the camera with her, she doubted it would work outside the house. If she was going to go back to Marcus, she had to go now. But how could she keep Caren from coming back in a matter of hours and calling out for her?

Quickly she picked up the phone, dialed Caren's number.

It was Jimmy who answered. "Hello?"

"Jimmy, is Caren around?"

Jimmy hesitated. "No. She had...some business in town to take care of."

Business with my doctors? Sarah wanted to ask, but she didn't. "Then will you give her a message for me?"

"Sure," he said. "What is it?"

"Tell her that I have to leave town for the weekend, to reshoot an ad that we've decided to change. I'll be back in a few days."

"Where are you going?" he asked, the concern in his voice growing more intense.

"It's just a little town in the northern part of the state. You've probably never heard of it."

"Sarah, are you sure you're up to this? I mean, you could get sick again...."

"I'm fine, Jimmy. Really. Please, tell Caren not to worry about me, okay? And tell her not to bother Mick with this. He doesn't know I screwed up this ad, and I want to fix it before he finds out."

Jimmy was quiet, as if not sure whether to believe her or not. "Couldn't it wait a few days? Just until you're stronger? I think Caren had some plans.... I mean, she wanted the two of you to do something to-morrow...."

Something like visiting a hospital? Talking to a doctor? Checking in for an extended stay?

"Tell her I'm sorry," Sarah said. "But I have to go now. And, Jimmy, tell her I love her, okay?"

Jimmy didn't answer as Sarah hung up the phone. She took a deep breath and went outside to move her car into the garage, where it couldn't be seen. Then she went back in, set the camera up on a tripod and said a prayer that her body could withstand the trip.

CHAPTER THIRTEEN

Marcus was prepared when he found Sarah this time, balled up on his dining room floor, looking already dead and wasted away. He had bought his own IV to keep at home and stocked up on the necessary drugs, and two days ago he'd gotten his medical equipment out of storage and set it all up in his bedroom. A mechanical respirator was stacked to one side, as well as a small heart monitor, a blood-pressure gauge and everything else he had imagined he might need in the worst possible case.

She had lost weight, he thought as he lifted her and ran to his bed with her. She had been sick a long time, probably since her last visit, and now she had voluntarily put herself through the trauma again. He felt for her pulse, saw how erratic it was, and quickly gave her an injection. Then, as quickly as a MASH doctor in the midst of a bloody catastrophe, he set up the IV and fed more medicine through the needle in her arm.

Sarah didn't move.

He felt her head, realized she was scalding with fever, and ran to get the ice he'd collected every day, just in case that would be the day she came back. It had melted together and was hardened into a block, so he got the hammer he kept beside the block and banged it until it was crushed into chunks he could pack around her.

It was only then that he was able to step back and look at her and realize how close she was hovering to death's door. He might lose her this time, and if he didn't, she might die on the trip home. This would have to be her last visit here. There was no way he could ever let her do this to herself again.

He sat down, helpless and weary, and as tears overcame him, he wept for the hopeless irony their lives had become.

It was three days later when Sarah woke. During that time, Marcus had kept full-time watch over her, barely keeping her alive with medicines and ice and constant care. Three days of holding his breath, waiting for her to take her last one. Three days of praying more earnestly than he'd ever prayed in his life.

And then she opened her eyes and looked right into his, and he was so profoundly moved by that small miracle that he dissolved into tears once again, clinging to her hand and stroking her face. She wasn't awake for long. Soon she drifted back into sleep, her fever still burning and her body still as weak as a sick kitten's.

It was then that Marcus dropped to his knees and made a promise to God that he knew he had no choice but to keep. *Spare her life, God, and I'll be content to grow old without her. Take her away from me . . . just let her live.*

And as she grew stronger and more conscious and more alive, he had to face the fact that this was the very last time he would ever know the peace of holding her.

"How much time do we have?" he asked her the next day, as she was just beginning to sit up in bed.

"I don't know," she said. "I left my sister a message that I was going out of town for a few days. I think I covered my bases pretty well, but she'll come looking for me soon."

She looked down at her food and told herself that it wasn't wise to eat much. Her stomach was still queasy. Her hands trembled as she moved a piece of toast around on her plate.

"You've lost weight," Marcus said. "At least fifteen pounds. How sick were you the last time?"

She averted her eyes, trying to shrug off the question. "I don't know. They make such a big thing out of it each time, and I finally had to just leave the hospital...."

"You left without their releasing you?"

"I had to." She closed her eyes and leaned her head back against the pillows he'd stacked at her back. "Caren was taking the camera."

Marcus's voice was strained. "Why? Did you tell her about all this?"

"No," she said, opening her eyes and meeting his again. "I couldn't. She would have freaked out and thought for sure I was crazy. But she started thinking I'd been exposed to something—radiation, I don't know. Or poisoned. And when she started snooping around, one of my friends, a guy I work with, told her about my playing with that camera. And she got it in her head that that was the problem."

"Oh, God. What was she going to do with it?"

"I don't know," she said. "Have it tested, destroy it. Who knows? So I had to leave the hospital. I had to get the camera back, and then I was scared that she'd done something to it that might have messed it up."

"Is that why you came back when you did? Even though your body wasn't ready?"

She looked at him fully. "How do you know my body wasn't ready?"

"Because you're wasting away, Sarah. You've lost too much weight, and you look sicker than I've ever seen you. What you're doing to yourself...it's not good. You must know that. Did you come back to see if the camera still worked?"

"No," she whispered. "I was trying to build my strength back before I did." Tears burst to her eyes, and she covered her face with a trembling hand. "I think she was making plans to have me committed. She thinks I'm crazy, Marcus. I couldn't take the chance of being put in a hospital I couldn't get out of, and not being able to get back to you."

He slipped his arms around her and held her while she cried, and after a moment she felt him shaking against her. Looking up, she saw that he was crying, too. Softly she touched his face. "Marcus, are you all right?"

He swallowed and shook his head. "You're killing yourself, Sarah. A little at a time. You've got to stop coming here...or I don't know what might happen to you."

She shook her head, but he set her back and shook her. "Do you hear me? I mean it, Sarah. If the return home doesn't kill you, then the next trip will. You can't do it. You have to promise me."

Sarah shook her head violently. "I can't promise that."

"You have to, damn it!" he shouted. "Promise me."

"No, Marcus! That's asking too much!" She broke into stronger sobs, and he held her against him again.

"Please, Sarah. Please don't come back to me."

She broke away from him this time, got out of bed and wobbled across the room. "I can't...I can't talk about this right now. I don't know how much time we have. There's so much for us to do. So many things..."

She staggered and caught herself, clutching the wall, and Marcus was beside her in an instant. He caught her as she started to faint and sat down with her, holding her tightly in his lap.

"I hate this," she whispered, dropping her head against his shoulder. "It's so unfair."

"I know, baby," he said into her hair. "I know."

"And what's going to happen to you, Marcus? I've only made your life worse, and I already know how it ends. You waste your life away grieving over all your past injustices, and you die a lonely old hermit with nothing but an obsession to your name."

Marcus was quiet as he held her, letting her weep out her heart, and finally he made her look up at him.

"What if...what if I made it end differently this time?"

"How?" she asked. "How could you?"

"I could try...to become something. To stop sitting around in this house, waiting for lightning to strike.... What if I promised you that?"

She wiped at her tears, but more were quick to follow. "What would you be, Marcus? A doctor again?"

"No, not that," he said. "But maybe go into research. My mother died of tuberculosis, and ever since I've wanted to work in that field, try to find a cure. They're doing segmental resections now, where they remove the infected lobe of a lung. I wouldn't do the surgery anymore, but I could be in on studying how effective that is, and what some other possible cures are. Is there a cure for TB in your time, Sarah?"

"Yes," she said. "But I don't know what it is." She stared at him for a moment, watching the illumination in his eyes as he thought of the possibilities. "Marcus, if you find that field so exciting, why don't you get into the surgical part of it? Why do you have to throw away something that you used to love, just because of one mistake?"

"Because," he said, too sternly, "I just can't, that's all. The point is, I won't live a miserable life. I'll *do* something. And maybe I won't run out in front of that car this time. Maybe, knowing what I know, I'll live, and you and I can know each other again...."

"But you'll be an old man," she wept. "You'll be at the end of your life."

"We don't have a choice!" he said. "Don't you see, you're at the end of your life *now,* if you keep coming back! Don't make me live the rest of my life knowing that you died because of me. I have enough death on my conscience.''

She caught her breath on another sob, but there was nothing she could say to that. He was right.

"I want to have you moved," she whispered, touching his face. "Your body."

"What?"

"To the little church cemetery. I found your parents' headstones, Marcus, and I started to clean them up. I think your body should be there with them."

He closed his eyes. "Where did they put me?"

"In some little nondescript grave, with just a little wooden cross to mark it. Oh, Marcus, I can't live with that. Will you take me to the cemetery, and let me see the little church, and how it used to look, and maybe I can put it back. Maybe I can restore that one little thing. It's not much, but— Oh, Marcus, it's all I've got."

He held her, knowing that she understood their plight, knowing that, even though she hadn't made the promise he needed from her, she understood the need for it. When she left this time, he thought, it would be the last time. And he'd have to wait more than forty years to see her again.

That night, he slept in the same bed with her, no longer afraid for her fever or her palpitations, and when they made love, it was gently, sweetly, for she was so weak he couldn't demand much from her. It was the most loving love they'd ever made, and they didn't let go of each other all night long.

The next day, he stayed in bed with her all day, knowing she was too weak to get up. He read to her from the newspaper, and she laughed and made comments about things that she knew would happen next. Then he played some records on his record player, and she told him about stereos and CDs and warned him to watch for Joni Mitchell and James Taylor in twenty years, and to listen to the words, because they would remind him of her.

"And if you invest in oil, get out during the seventies, before the bottom falls out of the market," she said, "but IBM will be a great investment, and so will Apple. And don't paint with lead-based paint. And be careful with asbestos."

He didn't know that Apple wasn't something one ate, and the concept of home computers was hard for him to grasp.

He moved his dusty, rarely watched television into the bedroom, and they watched in black-and-white as Lucy stomped grapes for wine, and Bud had a crisis that only Robert Young could solve on *Father Knows Best.*

She told him about docudramas and home videos, cable TV and big screens. He told her about listening to the crickets late at night on the back porch, hearing the birds sing early in the mornings, hearing the music of the wind, watching the comedy of the squirrels frolicking in his backyard.

And she admitted that she liked his entertainment better than anything available in her own decade.

As her energy returned, they made love with more fervor, more passion, and she loved him with everything she had. And she knew that each time they made love they were one step closer to never seeing each other again.

Sarah felt well enough the next day to get dressed in the clothes she had left here the last time and venture outside the house. The sunshine felt good to her, just the way it had in her own time under the same sky. Marcus drove her to the little church she'd wanted to see, and as they pulled into the small gravel parking lot she read the brightly painted sign: Holy Cross Baptist Church.

"It looks so sweet," she whispered. "In my day, it's boarded up and rotting, like some kind of crack house."

Marcus glanced over at her. "Sometimes it feels like we speak a different language. What's a crack house?"

"A place where lowlifes sell drugs," she said. "Can we go in, Marcus?"

"Sure," he said. "Come on."

He helped her out of the car, and they went to the double doors at the front of the small building. As he opened one and she saw the inside inviting her into its warmth, she was struck with a sense of belonging somehow, of fitting in. A sense of rightness.

He held her hand as they went in, and her eyes grew soft and wide as she slowly absorbed it all.

The sanctuary was painted white, from the altar to the pews, and the floor was hardwood and polished, as if someone who really loved the little building took care of it. A stained-glass window with a cross and a dove hung behind the small choir loft, and Sarah wondered if that window still hung in the old abandoned building in her time, or if it had been vandalized and forgotten.

"It's so beautiful," she whispered, afraid of spoiling the reverence with irreverent tones.

"Yes, it is," he said, sitting in the front pew and pulling her down beside him. "I haven't been here since before Korea." He frowned, and said, "Come to think of it, the last time was my father's funeral. That was pretty rough."

She looked up at him. "Your parents both died young. It must have been hard on you."

"Was," he said. "Mama died of TB...a real miserable death...and my father never seemed to get over it. He really depended on her for everything. When she died, he was lost. I think he spent the rest of his life just waiting to join her."

"What did he die of?"

"Heart attack," he whispered. A slow smile came to his lips, and he focused on the stained-glass window. "You should have seen them when I was a kid. So much in love. They used to have parties and dance all night. My folks could tear up the dance floor like nobody's business."

Sarah smiled. "I never knew my parents."

Marcus's smile faded. "Why not?"

"They died in a car crash over on Main Street when Caren and I were babies. My aunt and uncle raised us." She paused, stared off and added, "I never really missed them, because my aunt and uncle were good to us until they died. They were older when they got us, and I always wondered what it would have been like to be raised by a younger couple."

"You could meet them, you know."

Sarah gave Marcus a stricken look, as if the thought had never occurred to her. "They're probably teenagers now. Going to school, football games . . ." Her eyes filled with tears, and she whispered, "Do you think so, Marcus?"

"I don't know why not," he said. "We could start looking now. In the phone book, then find their addresses."

She was quiet for a moment, then whispered, "Not yet. Let's just sit here for a little longer. Listen."

"Listen to what?"

"To God's quiet. He talks to you through that quiet sometimes, you know."

Marcus smiled as she got quiet herself, listening to that sound that he'd never heard before, that music that he knew would forever be significant to him.

"You're really special, you know that?" he whispered, touching her pale face.

"You are," she said.

"No, I mean it. You have such a poignant way of seeing things. Mine is so dismal."

"You just need some happiness in your life," she whispered. "Then you'd see things differently."

"I see things differently already," he said, squeezing her hand and bringing it to his heart. "But it's hard to be happy when you know the very thing that has brought you happiness is about to be taken from you."

"Let's not talk about that," she whispered, laying her head against his shoulder. "Let's talk about what it would be like if I could stay here with you. What would we do?"

"The first thing," he said, dropping a kiss on her forehead, "would be to get married. Right here, if you wanted."

"Oh, Marcus," she said, her eyes brightening. "That would be so wonderful. And would we have children?"

"Children..." he said on a sigh. "I've never even thought of having children."

"But wouldn't you want them?"

"I would have," he said, his smile fading. "If you could have stayed."

Determined not to let him sink back into his depression, she pressed on. "We'd have to get married at daybreak," she whispered. "I'll bet the sun shines through that window right at daybreak, and it would light us in such a way that we'd feel touched by the very hand of God. Of course, if there were some way that I could stay, we'd know we were blessed that way, wouldn't we?"

"Yes." She wasn't making him feel better, for his depression grew keener with each facet of her fantasy. Finally she grew quiet.

"I love you, Marcus."

He closed his eyes. "I love you, too, baby. More than you could ever know. More than two lifetimes could hold."

Again they listened to the quiet, but finally, after a while, he whispered, "Please don't come back, Sarah. I mean it. Promise me you won't."

When she didn't answer, he tried again. "You'll die, baby. I know you think you won't, but you will."

"But you're a good doctor," she whispered. "I have faith in you."

"Don't," he said. "Death is death. I can't bring you back from it, no matter how hard I try. No matter how much I want to. And, God help me, I can't stand the thought that someone on the other side might not have the experience or the desire to bring you around if the return trip almost kills you."

"We have a good hospital. Good doctors," she whispered.

"Even the best doctors make mistakes," he said sadly. "Even the most dedicated lose heart and quit trying quite as hard as they once did. What's one more life, when there are so many others who have a better chance?"

"We aren't talking about war, Marcus," she whispered. "It'll be okay."

"This time, maybe. But there can't be a next time. I mean it, Sarah. You have to swear to me that you won't come back again. This is going to have to be goodbye."

Tears filled her eyes and rolled down her cheeks as she tried to go back to pretending that his life wasn't only in yesterday, and hers only in tomorrow. There had to be a now, even if it was only for a moment more. And she was going to hang on to it as long as she could.

* * *

Their search for Sarah's parents was steeped in somberness, for neither could shake the feeling of despair creeping over them as time ticked by. But Sarah had no trouble finding her maternal grandparents' address, for it was the same house they'd died in, when she was no more than ten.

Marcus drove her to the house, and she gazed at it from where they parked across the street. The house was pink, with freshly painted white shutters and a little flower garden that ran along the front walk.

"This is weird," she said, staring at the house where she'd eaten fresh-baked cookies and applesauce, where people had delighted in her and lavished her with love, where she had played with the little parakeet her grandma had kept in a cage in the kitchen. "My mother could be in there, but I have this strange feeling that I shouldn't talk to her. That it could reverse this whole time thing somehow. I haven't even been born yet." Her voice faded off, and finally she whispered, "Besides, who would I tell her I am?"

"You could make up something," he said. "But not if it would mess things up, Sarah. Let's not take any chances."

"I can't explain it," she whispered. "I just know that it would."

The front door opened, and a woman stepped out to sweep off the porch. Sarah sat up straight and strained to see. "Grandma!" she whispered. "She looks so young."

Marcus glanced over at her and saw tears burning her eyes.

Self-conscious, Sarah wiped the tear off her face. "Oh, Lord. I didn't realize how much I missed her."

A Ford came up the street and turned into her driveway, and Sarah didn't take her eyes off it as a teenage boy got out and walked around the car. Waving at her grandmother, he opened the door, and a girl of about sixteen bounced out, her skirt bobbing over her petticoat. Her dark hair was pulled back in a ponytail, and as she chewed gum, she blew a bubble, popped it and started up the steps.

"My mother," Sarah whispered.

"Are you sure?" he asked. "I thought she'd be a little younger."

"No," Sarah said. "She was in her late twenties when she had us. She and my father were married before they turned twenty, but she had trouble getting pregnant. Then, wham—twins." A poignant smile started in her eyes, then slowly made its way to her mouth. "Oh, Marcus, isn't she pretty? I wish Caren could see her."

The boy loped up the steps and plopped down next to her on the porch swing. He turned toward them and tossed a rock at a birdhouse on the lawn, missed, then put his arm around the girl.

"My father," Sarah said, astounded. "I recognize him from his picture! I knew they'd dated a long time before they got married, but I didn't realize they started this young!"

Marcus squeezed her hand tighter. "That's Kevin Rhinehart," he said. "He used to be one of my patients. I treated him for a broken leg right before I left for Korea."

"Really?" she asked. "What was he like?"

"He was a rascal," Marcus said on a soft chuckle. "But a good boy. He had the sharpest wit I'd ever seen in a kid his age, and he hated to admit he was sick—ever. Tough patient, but I liked him a lot." He glanced back at the boy, and his smile faded. "A car crash, huh? That's too bad."

"Yeah," she whispered, and her tears came more freely. "It is too bad."

They sat quietly for a long moment as the young couple flirted and laughed on the porch, but finally her grandmother came back out and called her daughter to supper.

Sarah watched as her father gave her mother a sweet parting kiss, then scuffed back to his car and drove away.

When there was no one left to watch, Sarah turned back to Marcus. "Thank you, Marcus. That meant so much to me."

"I know," he whispered.

And as they drove home, she could see that he was struggling just as hard as she with the emotions storming through them.

It was after midnight, after she and Marcus had made poignant love and fallen asleep entwined in each other's arms, that Sarah heard the voice in the distance, calling her from her sleep, waking her. She stirred and saw that Marcus still slept.

Sarah! The voice came again, stronger, and suddenly awareness drifted into her subconscious. She was going now, and there was nothing she could do to stop it.

"Marcus!"

He sat up abruptly, startled by her urgency, and tightened his hold on her. "She's calling, isn't she?"

Sarah!

"Oh, God, Marcus! I don't want to go!"

She touched his face, kissed him one last time and felt herself beginning to fade away. His hands slipped through her, but his eyes still locked on hers.

"Sarah, listen to me! Don't come back, do you hear me? Don't come back, or you'll die!"

"Marcus!"

"I mean it, Sarah!" he cried. "Don't do it. I love you, Sarah. I love you."

And before she could return the love to him, blackness descended on her again.

CHAPTER FOURTEEN

The hospital monitors beeped and flashed, and Caren checked the IV feeding her sister intravenously to make sure it was working properly. She'd learned more than she'd ever wanted to know about medicine during this past week, but she'd never expected to find her sister on the threshold of death, so deep in a coma that they didn't know if she'd ever wake up.

Sarah still burned with fever, even after a week and all the drugs they could give her, and occasionally she convulsed, frightening Caren so much that Jimmy had to relieve her. At other times, she had babbled incoherently, in half-muttered words Caren couldn't understand. Those times were the worst, for they gave Caren false hope that Sarah was coming back, that she would wake up and fuss about all the tubes and machines, ask for something to eat and insist on going home.

But she feared those days would never come again.

She settled back in her chair, watching her sister with weary eyes. The doctors hadn't yet pinpointed what was wrong with Sarah, though they were throwing around possibilities like encephalitis, meningitis, and a number of terminal diseases that Caren couldn't even allow herself to consider. Poison or radiation exposure still hadn't been ruled out, either. Whether she would recover from this bout was doubtful, but Caren hadn't given up hope.

She heard a whisper from her sister's lips and leaned forward, shaking Sarah slightly. "Sarah? Are you awake?"

"Marcus," Sarah whispered, her face beginning to glisten as a fine perspiration coated her skin. "Marcus, hold me."

"Marcus?" Caren sat back, staring at her sister in disbelief. Why would she be calling out Marcus's name? "Sarah, you're just dreaming, honey. Wake up. Wake up and talk to me."

"Caren."

The word was the first hope she'd had in days, and she caught her breath as her heart stumbled into a breakneck cadence. "Yes, honey. I'm here. Come on, Sarah, wake up. You're almost there."

"I didn't die, Marcus. I'm alive."

"No, honey, you didn't die. You're gonna be fine."

Sarah's face twisted, and she whispered, "But you keep calling me back."

"I have to," Caren whispered. "You have to wake up, Sarah."

"But I wanted to stay with him."

"With whom, Sarah?"

"Marcus," Sarah whispered weakly. "Oh, Caren, he's so wonderful, and he loves me so much, and it's all so unfair."

Her words came on a barely audible breath, but they were coherent enough that there was no mistaking them. "Honey, Marcus is dead. He was an old man...."

"Not in 1953, he wasn't. That's where I've been, Caren. In 1953, with Marcus."

For a moment, Sarah's words stunned Caren into silence, and she gaped at her sister, wondering if coherency was a common trait in comas. Mumbling nonsense was one thing, but forming sentences, dates, names...that was another.

"Marcus...Stephens?" she asked. "Sarah, are you talking about Marcus Stephens?"

"Yes," Sarah whispered. "And I saw Mama and Daddy, and they were teenagers.... But you always call me back, Caren. And I get so sick...."

"How?" Caren asked. "How do I call you back?"

"When you come into the house and you call out my name, it brings me back through time...." Her voice faded out, and for a moment Caren thought she had gone back to sleep. "But it's so traumatic," she went on suddenly. "He says I'll die if it happens again. I'm afraid I'll die if it doesn't."

Caren struggled to put Sarah's words together, make some sense of any of what she said. Traveling through time, being called back, winding up sick?

"How do you get there, Sarah?" she asked, hoping that keeping her sister talking would prevent her from slipping back into the oblivious state she'd been in.

"Camera," Sarah whispered, her words growing slower and more difficult. "Sends me there. Don't know how."

"And I call you back?"

"Yes. Every time."

Caren stroked her hair back from her clammy forehead and discovered that the fever had broken. "Sarah, you haven't been with Marcus, honey. You've been hallucinating while you were sick. And if I've been calling you back, it's from this coma you've been in. And I'm going to keep calling you back, as long as it takes to bring you all the way back."

"But I was so happy with him there," she whispered, and one lone tear slipped down her temple. "So happy."

"But it was a dream, honey." Caren touched the tear, felt the warmth of it, and new tears filled her own eyes. "I wish I could make it true for you. I wish I could give you that soul mate you've been yearning for and tell you that you really have been with someone who makes you happy. If there was any way in the world I could give it to you, even if it meant giving up my own happiness, I'd do it, honey."

"You could, Caren," Sarah whispered.

"How?"

"Next time, don't call me back. Just let me go and know that I belong there . . . with him."

The impact of her words shook Caren's soul, and her nose reddened as more tears pushed to her eyes. "I can't do that, Sarah. I can't just abandon you to this coma. You're going to walk out of here, damn it, no matter how comfortable it feels to get lost there."

As if there were no way to make her sister understand, Sarah shook her head weakly and fell into a quiet sleep again.

* * *

It was midnight when Sarah woke the next time and found Caren curled up in Jimmy's lap on the little vinyl couch beside her bed. They were both asleep, keeping vigil over her, and she looked down at herself and realized that she was attached to all sorts of life-support systems, monitors, tubes and IVs.

She glanced around, saw the glass wall of her room and the nurses milling around outside. She was in ICU, she thought. Marcus had been right. She'd almost died.

"Caren?"

Caren woke instantly, and Jimmy stirred, as well. In a second, Caren was beside her. "Sarah, are you awake?"

"How long have I been in here?" Sarah asked weakly.

She didn't understand the depth of Caren's sigh of relief at her having asked a coherent question. "About a week. Oh, God, Jimmy, she's really awake this time! Sarah, how do you feel?"

"Lousy. I feel like a sledgehammer has been pounding my head, and my throat feels on fire." She closed her eyes again and tried to fathom what had happened to her. "A week? Really?"

"You've been in intensive care all this time, but I've been right here with you, in case you woke up. Oh, you have no idea how scared we were. And then all the false alarms, when I thought you were awake but you weren't. Hallucinating about Marcus Stephens and Mama and Daddy..."

Sarah caught her breath. "I told you that?"

"Oh, yeah, among other things. It was crazy, and I kept thinking if I just kept you talking, you'd snap out of it, but you just kept dreaming...."

Sarah closed her eyes and realized that she might very well have told Caren everything. Even about the camera. What if Caren went back and got it?

Tears came to her eyes as she realized that it almost didn't matter. Marcus was right. One more trip would kill her. She was stuck here, and he was stuck there, and now he was dead and she would never have the chance to see him again.

Caren touched her hand. "Sarah, what's wrong?"

Sarah shook her head. "Nothing. I'm just so tired of being sick. What are they saying is wrong with me?"

"Still just a virus," Caren lied. "But they're going to get it altogether this time. You're going to be just fine."

Sarah wiped her tears, tried to pull herself together. Finally she forced herself to look into her sister's eyes. Caren's eyes were red and tired, and Sarah knew she probably hadn't left her side since they'd brought her in. "I love you," she whispered.

"Me, too," Caren said. "I'm so glad you're back."

Sarah closed her eyes and tried to forget just where she was back from. It didn't pay to remember, and yet she knew she always would. How did one just let go of a passion so real that it consumed both body and mind, that it obsessed and possessed, that it gave life even as it was killing her?

It couldn't happen, she thought, so she was destined to go through life with only those memories.

Still, she knew that that was better than never having known Marcus at all.

It was two weeks, this time, before Sarah was able to leave the hospital. When she finally did, she had lost ten more pounds, and her clothes hung from her small body. Caren had gone shopping for her and bought her some new things, but Sarah had little interest in them.

"I've packed a bag for you," Caren told her as she drove her home from the hospital. "I want you to stay with Jimmy and me for a couple of weeks...until your strength is back."

Sarah gave her a disturbed look. "Caren, no. I want to go home."

"You can't go home," Caren said. "Honey, you're so weak, you can barely walk."

"I'm fine," she said. "And I'll take it easy, I swear. Just...please take me home."

Caren got that stubborn look on her face. "No, Sarah. At the moment, I'm stronger than you, and if I have to physically drag you into my house, you're staying with me."

Sarah felt that tragic, debilitating helplessness again, and she dropped her head back on the headrest. "All right," she said finally. "But can't we go by there...just for a while? I...have some things I need to get."

Caren glanced over at her. "All right, I guess it wouldn't hurt."

Sarah was quiet for the rest of the drive, wondering what Marcus was doing, if he had stopped looking for her, if he was worried that she had died. She supposed he would never have any way of knowing.

They reached her house, and she felt that old stirring of homecoming, only she knew it wasn't the old structure that made her feel that way, but the memory of Marcus inside it. The rooms were all the same, and the light came through the windows exactly as it had in his time. But there was one vital difference.

Marcus wasn't here.

Tears poured down her face, and she smeared them away as she and Caren got out of the car. Slowly she walked up the porch steps to the front door, unlocked it and went inside.

The house was dark and dusty, and she turned on a light and went to a window to open the front curtain. A light blinked on her answering machine, and she thought how she wanted to get rid of it as soon as possible. She wanted to get back to a simpler life, the way it had been in Marcus's day. No machines that dictated her life. No running just to stay in place.

"Sarah?"

Sarah turned around and saw her sister leaning back against her dining room table, watching her with concern in her eyes. "Are you sure you're okay?"

"Yeah," she said. "It's just weird, that's all. Coming back here."

"Why? Because you've been in the hospital so long?"

"Yeah," she said, but she knew it had more to do with the life that Marcus had brought to the house. "Have you ever been in my attic?"

Caren frowned. "No, why?"

"Because there's a chair up there. An old easy chair, right by the gable window. I found out that one of the people who owned the house before was going to make a bedroom up there, and he started to fix it up so he could rent out part of the house. Then he changed his mind. The chair's still there...."

Caren waited for some pertinent tie-in to what was going on today, but none came. "How did you find that out?"

"Doesn't matter," Sarah whispered, looking out the window. The light cast dark shadows on one side of her face, and Caren thought she looked so waiflike, so alone. Then Sarah turned back to her again. "You were going to have me committed, weren't you?"

Caren stood straighter, bracing herself for a turn in the conversation that she hadn't expected at all. "No, Sarah. I've just been worried about you, and I wanted—"

"You were going to check me into a psychiatric hospital, weren't you?" Sarah's voice was calm, unaccusing. "It's okay, Caren. I don't blame you."

"Is that why you left?"

Sarah nodded. "I'm not crazy, Caren."

"I know you're not," Caren said softly, coming toward her. "But you've been so sick. And your obsessions lately with that Marcus guy and those graves and all the sudden trips and the discrepancies in where you've been. I thought maybe there was brain damage, or that you had some sort of neurological disorder that wasn't too far gone to be corrected." Tears came to Caren's eyes, and she blinked them back.

"Believe it or not, sis, I wanted to help you. I was desperate to help you."

"I know you were."

"Then tell me how," Caren said. "Tell me what to do."

Sarah looked down at her hands for a long moment, then finally faced her sister again. "You know those things you said I told you when I was in the coma?"

Caren nodded. "About being with Marcus in some other time?"

"Yes," she whispered. "Caren, what if I hadn't been hallucinating? What if I'd been awake at the time, and it was true?"

Caren shrugged. "Well...it couldn't be. Think about it."

Sarah kept her eyes locked on her sister's face. "But use your imagination for a minute. Sometimes strange things happen, things that no one can understand or explain. UFO sightings, out-of-body experiences, even the telepathy you and I have had at different times in our lives."

"But, Sarah, we're talking about time travel. It couldn't happen."

"But what if it could?" Sarah asked again. "For just a minute, suspend your disbelief. Think about what it would have been like, if it really had happened."

Confusion was rampant on Caren's face. "What *what* would have been like?"

"What I told you. What if I really *had* traveled back through time somehow and found Marcus? What if all the things that had happened were just part of a cycle? What if I fell in love with him, in another time, but I couldn't stay, because you were the only one on this earth with the power to call me back, and you kept doing it, over and over and over?''

Caren brought her hand to her forehead and began to massage her temple. "Sarah, I don't understand what you're saying. Is that what you think happened?''

"It doesn't matter what I think happened," Sarah said. "Just picture it. Imagine it and let go of what you know to be fact.''

Caren looked helplessly at her. "I can't, Sarah. It's crazy.''

"Yes, it's crazy, isn't it?" Sarah said. "But, oh, what if it could have been true! And what if I had to make a choice to stay there...with him...if I could ever make it back again? How could I make you stop calling me back?''

"You couldn't," Caren said, her face twisting. "As long as you're alive, I'll keep fighting for you.''

"Why?" Sarah asked, almost frantically.

"Because I love you, Sarah. I can't lose you.''

"But what if I was in a better place? Someplace I wanted to be with all my heart? What if I felt more like I belonged there than here? What if I had found there something I've never found here? If you understood that, would you still keep calling me back?''

Caren collapsed into a chair, as if she'd given up on making sense of her sister's words. "Oh, Sarah, if you're asking me to let you die next time, I won't do it. Don't ask me to do that, because I can't.''

Sarah went to her and knelt down in front of her, intent on making her understand. "I'm not asking you to let me die, Caren," she whispered. "I'm asking you to let me live. Let me go."

But she saw in Caren's tormented eyes that she still couldn't understand, and as Caren broke into sobs, Sarah reached her thin arms around her and held her tightly. "I'll always love you, Caren, even if I'm not with you. But I want someone of my own."

"I want that for you, too," Caren cried.

"Then trust me to find it my own way," she whispered.

Caren nodded, as if she would trust, as if she believed, but Sarah knew that in the back of her sister's mind she harbored the doubt that Sarah was even sane. What she had just told her, instead of clarifying everything, had only served to upset her more.

Finally Sarah got to her feet, suddenly feeling wearier than she ever had. "I'll go gather up some things and we can go," she said.

Caren didn't answer, and Sarah went into the darkroom to get Marcus's box. There was no way Caren would allow her to take it with her, but she reached in and pulled out the snapshots of him. Tears came to her eyes as she looked at each of them in turn, then slid them into her pocket.

She looked up and saw the tripod still standing in the corner of the room. But the camera was gone.

Her heart began to pound, faster than it had been able since her last trip back, and she looked frantically around. "Caren!" she called, panicked.

Caren was at the door in an instant.

"Where's the camera?" she asked, whirling around.

Caren glanced around at the various cameras and lenses in their cases all over the room. "Which one?"

"You know which one!" Sarah said. "The old one! What did you do with it?"

"Oh." Caren took a deep breath and stepped farther into the room. "I have it at my house," she said. "Don't worry, I'm not going to hurt it. I just wanted Jimmy to test it for radiation. It's been set up here every time I've found you, and I can't help thinking that it's emitting something that's hurting you."

"We've been through this," Sarah said. "Caren, I want it back."

"Well, you're not going to get it," Caren said. "I mean it, Sarah. I've let you call the shots long enough. If it has anything to do with your illness, we're going to find out. Don't you want to know?"

Sarah tried to calm herself, but her hands trembled. "It's... Of course I want to know.... I just..."

"You don't want to keep making yourself sicker," Caren cut in. "If it has anything to do with the camera, then you shouldn't be around it."

"But..." She blinked back her tears, and the terror in her throat. "You wouldn't destroy it or anything? Or take it apart, looking for something?"

"I won't touch it," she said. "I've just put it up where you won't be tempted to play with it. And Jimmy's going to bring some radiation-detection equipment home to test it."

Sarah's heart didn't slow down, and she felt dizzy again and grabbed on to a wall. Perspiration dotted

her skin, and suddenly she felt Caren pulling her into
a chair and handing her a glass of water.

"Are you okay?"

"Yes." Sarah drank the water, then handed it back
to Caren before her trembling hands could spill it. She
closed her eyes and leaned her head back. Maybe
Caren was right about her being crazy, she thought.
She should be glad her sister had removed the camera
and all temptation to go back to Marcus, because she
knew even more vividly than Marcus did that going
back would kill her.

But what if it didn't?

The tiny thought kept playing in the back of her
mind, over and over, like a chant. What if it didn't kill
her? What if she had the strength left for one more trip
and made sure before she left that she would never be
called back again? Would it be worth risking death,
just for the chance to spend a lifetime with Marcus?

Yes, she thought, it would be worth it. All she had
to do was figure out a way.

CHAPTER FIFTEEN

Sarah tried to put the camera out of her mind for the next couple of weeks, while her sister pampered and nursed her back to health. But sometimes she couldn't help herself. She found herself cleaning Caren's house mercilessly, straightening shelves and closet tops, all the while searching for the machine that would transport her back to Marcus for the final time. But she couldn't find it.

She went home every day, under the pretense of taking care of business she'd let slide since her illness. The real reason was that it made her feel closer to Marcus. It was his house as much as hers, and though the furnishings were different, his aura still seemed to linger in every room.

Daily she climbed up to the attic, sat in the dusty, torn chair that Marcus had put up there himself over forty years ago, hugged her knees and gazed out the gable window, trying to recall his face and the way he had held her, the special fit of their bodies against each other, the scent of his skin....

And then she cried over all the things that could have been between them, all the things that could have been different in their lives, all the happiness wasted, all the joys she would never know.

In an effort to feel as if she were doing something for him, Sarah called her Realtor and asked her to find out who owned the boarded-up church around the corner. She wanted to buy it, she told her, so that she could renovate it.

"What are you going to do with it?" the Realtor asked.

Sarah hesitated. "I don't know yet," she said. "But it's there, and it should be taken care of, don't you think?"

The Realtor called back less than a week later and told her that the building had been foreclosed on years before, and the bank was more than willing to sell it to her for a song.

"Does that include the graveyard?" she asked.

"Well, yes," the Realtor said. "But if that's a problem, we could probably arrange to have the graves removed."

"No," she said quickly. "I want it just like it is."

They made arrangements to set the date of the closing, and Sarah cashed in a CD her aunt had left her and prepared to write the check for the church.

The day of the closing, Caren tried to keep her from leaving her house. "Sarah, this is a lot of money to throw away. Are you sure you want to do this?"

"Positive," she said. "Why does it bother you so much?"

"Because it's one of those obsessive things again. It has something else to do with that Marcus guy."

"Maybe it's just because I like old buildings," she said. "Maybe it's because I see a lot of wonderful potential there, and I think it's disgraceful that it's been neglected so badly." She gathered her purse, her checkbook and the necessary papers for the closing and started for the door. "Besides, Caren, I've been thinking about opening a studio. Maybe slowing down a little, so I don't have to travel so much. I could set it up there."

"In a church, with a graveyard out back?"

"Why not?"

"It's morbid, Sarah, that's why!"

"Oh, Caren. It's not morbid. It's sweet. You should walk through the graveyard sometime. Since I've been cleaning it up, I've found so many interesting stories. A little girl who died of cholera at two. An old man who had seventy grandchildren . . ."

"Was he related to Marcus?"

Sarah stopped at the door and turned back to her. "Caren, why does the thought of my thinking of Marcus bother you so much?"

"Because that's when all this started," Caren said. "You haven't been the same since."

"I haven't been the same because I've been sick," she lied. "One thing has nothing to do with the other."

Caren sighed. "Well, it's just weird. It's like you've adopted this dead person as your latest cause. Like you're going to carry on his work for him, or something crazy like that."

"Marcus didn't have any work to carry on," Sarah said. "He gave up everything that meant anything to him after Korea. His life just went downhill from there."

"So you're determined to make something more of it?"

Sarah looked at the floor. "Caren, I can't explain this to you. Your mind's closed so tight, you can't even let any light in."

"Or maybe yours is letting in so much that you're blinded by it."

Irritation tightened Sarah's chest. "Make up your mind, Caren. Am I blind or crazy?"

Caren stared at her, speechless, and finally Sarah forced herself to let go of her anger. "I love you, sis. No matter what you think of me." She started out of the house, but Caren stopped her. "Sarah."

Sarah turned around, bracing herself for more recriminations. But Caren only brought her hand to her lips, pressed a kiss on her palm and blew it to Sarah.

Smiling, Sarah pretended to catch it, and, holding it against her heart, as she'd done since they were children, she left the house.

Sarah didn't feel any better after she had the deed to the old church in her hand. It was still dilapidated, and most of the graves were still so overgrown that it would take her weeks, months, to clean them all up. She didn't have the money to hire anyone to do the renovations just yet, but that was all right, because she really wanted to do it all herself, anyway. It made her feel that she was doing something for Marcus, something important, and she vowed that once it was all finished, she would have him moved to that grave site.

Unless she could find that camera and try to go back to him again.

More and more, as she worked in the church and the graveyard behind it, she embraced the possibility that she was strong enough to go back to him one more time. Yes, she was still weak, but she grew stronger every day. And if there was even a chance...

The problem would be to find the camera.

She stayed at Caren's house longer than she needed to in the interest of finding the camera, and each night after Caren and Jimmy went to bed, she rifled through drawers and cabinets, their garage, their utility rooms, file cabinets, everything she could find, searching for it.

She had almost given up on finding it when she spotted the camera in the safe in Caren's wall—a safe hidden behind a painting, something she hadn't even known was there. Caren was opening it to get out an elegant necklace Jimmy had given her when Sarah saw the camera pushed to the back of the safe.

She turned around so that Caren wouldn't know she had seen it, but her heartbeat pounded like a trip-hammer as Caren locked the safe and dropped the key, attached to her key chain, back into her purse.

For the rest of that day, hope filtered through her heart, hope that she could get her hands on it again, that she could make one last trip to Marcus, that she could stay with him this time. But it wouldn't be easy to convince Caren to stop calling her. There was only one way to do that, one way that was almost too horrible to consider. But it was the only choice, and she had to take her chances where she could get them.

She waited until they went to bed, then got the key from Caren's purse and quietly opened the safe. Pulling out the camera, she stuffed it into her duffel bag with some of the clothes she'd brought over. Then, quickly, she locked the safe again, returned the key to Caren's purse and started for the door.

"Where are you going?"

She whirled around and saw Caren standing in the hallway, dressed in a pretty white gown that Sarah had given her for a wedding gift. Jimmy loved it, she'd said, and he especially loved taking it off of her. "Uh...nowhere," she said. "I mean...home. I couldn't sleep, and I decided I should try sleeping at home tonight."

"Just like that?" Caren asked. "Weren't you even going to tell me?"

"I just decided," she said. "I didn't want to wake you."

Caren cut across the room, looked down at the duffel bag in her hand. It looked heavier than it would have with just a few items of clothing. "Are you sure...that everything's all right?"

"Of course," Sarah said. "I'm fine."

"Well...all right, then. I guess I'll talk to you tomorrow."

Sarah looked at her sister, and suddenly she realized that if she went through with this, if her plan worked and she went back to Marcus, she would never see her again. Tears came to her eyes, and she reached out and touched her sister's face. "I love you, Caren. Thank you for taking care of me."

Tears came to Caren's eyes, as well, as though she sensed that some terrible thing was about to change her life. "You're my sister. What else would I do but take care of you?"

The idea of turning and going, of saying goodbye to her sister forever, was a little more difficult than Sarah had thought. She reached for Caren, pulled her into a hug and held her so tightly that she feared she wouldn't be able to let her go. "Caren, please... whatever happens... know that it's what I want."

Caren pulled back, a look of deep apprehension coloring her face. "What are you talking about? What's going to happen?"

Sarah backed up, wondering if she'd said too much. She wiped at her tears and tried to battle the sadness lodging itself in her heart. "Nothing, necessarily. I just mean... it hasn't been right here for me for a very long time, Caren. You know that... and when there's a chance, just a chance, to set things right... sometimes sacrifices have to be made. Terrible sacrifices."

"Oh, God." Caren threw her hands over her mouth, and her face reddened as tears rimmed her eyes. "Please, Sarah. Whatever you're gonna do, don't do it! It's not worth it."

Sarah caught her breath on a sob. "Caren, please listen to me. This is important."

Caren looked up at her, her shoulders shaking with her sobs.

"Have you ever been in the right place at the wrong time?"

"I don't know."

"Well, I have. I have the chance to set it right. And if one day I'm not around here for you to see and talk to everyday, it doesn't mean I'm not thinking about you, loving you, watching you...."

"Oh, God, Sarah," Caren squealed. "Please... suicide isn't the answer. We can get you help! We can work this out!"

Sarah's heart collapsed, and she stood before Caren, wanting with all her heart to make her understand that it wasn't suicide, but a rebirth, that would take her away. It was love of a dimension she had never experienced before. Love even greater than that of a sister for a sister.

The bedroom door opened, and Jimmy came out, and when he saw his wife's state, he put his arms around her. "What is it, sweetheart? What happened?"

"She's...gonna do it..." Caren cried. "She's...leaving...."

Jimmy looked at Sarah, who steadied herself against her own tears. "I just want to sleep in my own bed tonight," she said. "That's all."

"No," Caren said. "Jimmy, please don't let her go."

Jimmy held Caren and pressed her face against his T-shirt. "Sarah, can't you please stay? It can't be that important...."

Sarah racked her brain for some way to appease her sister, so that she could leave without having her come after her immediately, trying to divert her from her mission. If only she hadn't been caught leaving, she thought, she could have had it all over with by now.

But standing here, watching her sister's heart break, she couldn't walk away. Slowly she set down the duffel bag. "All right," she whispered. "If it means that much to you, Caren, I'll stay. Jimmy's right. It wasn't that important."

Caren sucked in a sob. "Yes, all right. Then... then you'll stay here, and... and I'll get you something to help you sleep, and then... then tomorrow we'll go see the doctor and we'll help you feel better, Sarah. I swear we will. Please, just give me the chance..."

"All right," Sarah whispered, reaching for Caren. Their embrace was desperate, urgent, terrified, and she couldn't help feeling every stab of her sister's pain, for it was her pain, as well. "I'll stay, Caren. Just stop crying."

Caren calmed enough to go to the kitchen and find her a mild over-the-counter sleeping pill, and she came back with a glass of water. "Here," she said. "Take this."

Sarah put the pill in her mouth and hid it under her tongue, then pretended to drink. "Thank you," she said. "I'll just go to bed. Surely I'll be asleep in a few minutes."

"Yeah, okay." Caren gave her one last look, then hugged her tightly again. "I love you, Sarah."

"I love you, too."

Sarah watched as Jimmy took Caren to their bedroom, and she quickly spit the pill out of her mouth. She lay down on her bed, staring at the ceiling. Right now, Jimmy was in there holding her, comforting her, loving her the way only a husband could love a wife. But Sarah would never know that kind of love again.

She lay there, crying, for more than an hour, waiting until she knew her sister was asleep. Finally she got up, grabbed her bag and sneaked out the front door.

No one ever knew she had gone.

She drove to her house, went in and quickly set up the camera on the tripod. Fighting the temptation to use it right away, she found a pen and a notepad. Sitting down in the quiet of her living room, she began to write.

Dear Caren,
I wish there were some way to explain this to you so that you'd understand.

But there wasn't, she told herself, chewing on the end of the pen and trying to decide what to write next. If she told her the truth, and by some fluke Caren believed her, she'd still call her back. She couldn't trust her not to.

There was only one way, she thought, even though she had already seen how it would break her sister. If Caren thought she was dead, she wouldn't try to call her back. If she never came into her house and called out her name, Sarah could stay with Marcus.

She dropped her head in her hands, and hot tears burned down her face as she realized how devastated Caren would be. But Jimmy would be there to hold her together. He would help her. And maybe, from the depths of Caren's subconscious, after it was all said and done, she'd know in her heart that the things Sarah had told her earlier were true, and that her sister wasn't dead…that she was happy, in another time.

If the trip back didn't kill her.

But she couldn't think about that right now. Marcus would save her. He had to.

She put the pen back to the paper and wrote more.

I've been so sick, and the pain doesn't go away. I try to fight it, but it gets worse instead of better. It's not worth it anymore. I'm tired of fighting something I can't change.

But it was too cruel, she thought, to plant the seed of suicide outright and let Caren think that it was the end of her. She had to give her more, she thought, without leaving a door open through which she could call her back. She thought for a moment, then tried again.

Caren, please don't grieve for me. When you despair, listen to your heart. The same heart that told you when I hurt myself as a child, the same heart that helps you read my mind sometimes, whether I want you to or not. Your heart will know the truth, and you can trust it. Your heart will tell you how much better off I am. Remember the things I've told you.

I love you, and I love Jimmy, and nothing will ever change that. Please try to understand....

Love, Sarah

It would wound Caren, she thought, but not mortally, for she knew that, after a few days of unutterable grief, Caren would consult her heart, and she'd know that what Sarah had said was true.

She folded the paper and put it in an envelope, then went back out to her car. Hurrying, she loaded her bicycle into her trunk, then got into the car.

She was back at Caren's ten minutes later, and, leaving her car idling on the street so it wouldn't wake them, she went up the porch steps and slipped the note under the door.

The impact of what she was doing hit her all at once, and she almost collapsed from the pain of it. She thought of banging on the door, grabbing the letter back and staying here, where she was safe, where her sister loved her. . . .

But she would have to live the rest of her life without Marcus.

Pulling herself together, she went back to her car and drove away.

She stopped on the bridge, got her bicycle out and parked it against the rail. Then, standing on the bridge, she looked out over the water. Caren would find the note first, and then she'd go after her. She would see the bicycle the moment she reached the bridge, and she would think Sarah had jumped.

She covered her face and wept for the cruel hoax fate had forced her to play. It was a terrible thing, yet she saw no alternative.

Still distraught, she got into her car and drove back home. By the time Caren came into this house again, she thought, she would think Sarah was dead. And there would be no reason for her to call out for her.

She set the timer on the camera, took her place on the stool in front of it, and, as she waited the sixty seconds it would take to change her life, she looked around at all the things she would be leaving....

And she knew, in spite of all the pain it would cause her sister and the risk it would mean to her own life, she was doing the only thing she could to set destiny right.

CHAPTER SIXTEEN

She was dead when he found her.

But death hadn't stopped Marcus in the MASH units of Korea, and he didn't take the time to collapse in grief, to wail or to gnash his teeth. Instead, he operated on pure instinct, doing immediate CPR, pumping her chest until he felt a pulse. . . .

He grabbed the phone, still holding her wrist, and with the hand holding the receiver he dialed out the number for an ambulance. "This is Dr. Stephens, at 525 West Oak Circle," he blurted. "I need an ambulance, stat. Cardiac arrest."

He felt her pulse weakening again, felt it skipping and wavering, and he threw the phone down and pumped her again. "Don't leave me, baby!" he said through his teeth as he worked. "You came back here for a reason. Damn it, don't you leave me!"

The ambulance was there in minutes, and, never once letting go of her, he ordered what he needed. Her pulse still faltered and skipped beats as he climbed into the ambulance, barking out orders for supplies and drugs they would need once they reached the hospital.

The paramedic checking her blood pressure called it out to him, and Marcus shook his head violently. "Damn it, Sarah, hold on! You've come this far!"

"We're losing her."

The paramedic's voice cut through his fear, and Marcus cried out, "The hell we are! She's gonna be all right! She has to be!"

It was 4:00 a.m. when Caren woke with the terrifying feeling that something was pressing down on her heart, smothering her, crushing her....

She sat bolt upright in bed, caught her breath and looked around her in the dark. Jimmy lay sleeping soundly beside her, undisturbed.

She shoved her hair back and realized her forehead was wet. Her gown, too, was damp with perspiration. Quickly she got out of bed and left the bedroom. The house was quiet, dark, and the door to the guest room, where Sarah slept, was closed. Quietly she tiptoed past it into the living room, poured herself a glass of ice water and drank, trying to fight the sensation of panic she'd awakened with, the feeling of death bearing down on her, the certainty that something terrible had happened.

Sarah. The thought came to her that Sarah was in some kind of physical distress at this very moment. Quickly she ran to the door, threw it open and prepared to wake her sister.

But Sarah wasn't there.

"Oh, God!" She threw her hand over her mouth and turned on the light. The bed had been slept in, and Sarah's things were still hanging in the closet where she had left them.

Slowly she backed out of the guest room and headed for the living room. Flicking on the light, she looked around, but no one was there.

That was when she saw the note lying on the floor beneath the front door.

Her breath was trapped in her chest as she bent down and picked it up. That panic rose inside her again, and she screamed out, "Jimmy!"

In seconds he was beside her, and she thrust the note at him. "She's killing herself. Jimmy, we've got to stop her!"

"Come on," he said, grabbing his keys. "We'll go stop her."

"What if it's too late?" she cried.

"It won't be," he said. "It can't be."

They ran barefoot to the car, Caren still wearing her gown, and Jimmy in a pair of gym shorts and a T-shirt. As they pulled out of the driveway, Caren's panic rose higher. "Oh, Jimmy, please hurry!"

He tore down the street, and up to the little bridge they always had to cross. The car went so fast that they didn't see the bike until they'd already passed it.

"Wait!"

Jimmy slammed on the brakes and backed the car up until his headlights shone on the bicycle leaning against the bridge. "Is that her bike?"

"Oh, God!" Caren got out of the car and looked frantically around for Sarah.

"Sarah!" Jimmy called. "Sarah, where are you?"

Caren had wilted against him, weeping in great sobs, unable to look for her. "She jumped," she said, sobbing against his shirt. "Oh, my God, she jumped...."

Jimmy stopped calling and held her, looking around them, waiting for Sarah to walk up and tell her sister it would be all right. But deep down, where logic reigned, he knew that Caren was right.

"We have to call the police," he whispered.

"No." Caren shook her head frantically and started back for the car. "Maybe she's at home," she said. "I know she's at home."

"But, Caren, the note. She told you what she was going to do. Her bike..."

"It could have been stolen," she said. "And she could have changed her mind. Maybe she's at home asleep in her own bed. Maybe she's fine—"

She broke down into sobs again, unable to finish, and he walked her back to the car. "We'll go check her house and call the police from there," he said. "It'll be all right, baby. She's probably there."

Caren got into the car next to him, trembling and clinging to him with all her might as they finished the drive to Sarah's house.

Sarah's car, parked in the drive, offered a sense of normalcy, and Caren found herself hoping, again, that her sister was there. But that very hope terrified her, for something deep within her told her that she wasn't going to find her there.

"I can't go in," she said, as Jimmy opened the car door and started to get out. "I... I can't."

"Are you afraid of how you might find her?"

"No," Caren cried. "I'm afraid of not finding her at all."

"I'll go," he said. "Just wait here."

Caren waited in the car, her heart pounding, praying that he would come back out with Sarah behind him, that Sarah would throw her arms around her and tell her she'd changed her mind, that there was something worth living for, that she wasn't going to end it all.

She waited too long for him to come back out, and finally, unable to stand it any longer, she got out of the car and went inside.

Jimmy was coming down the stairs, a doleful look on his face. "She's not here, sweetheart. I called the police. They're going to meet us at the bridge."

"Nooo!" She threw her hand over her mouth and collapsed back against the wall. "Oh, Jimmy..."

"Honey, maybe they'll find her. If she jumped, maybe she's still alive. Maybe..."

"No, she couldn't have jumped. She wouldn't have! We weren't brought up that way! Suicide isn't in our nature...."

"But she was sick, baby. Maybe she couldn't take it. You don't know what she might do...."

"No!" She tore out of his arms and ran to the kitchen, looked inside, then ran out to the bathroom. Jimmy came after her, allowing her to look in every room desperately seeking her sister.

Finally she came to the darkroom, and she switched on the light and went in. The camera was still set up on the tripod, the camera she had hidden, the camera that seemed to have some bearing on what kept happening to her sister.

"The camera!" she cried. "She found the camera. I had hidden it from her, and she— Oh, God, Jimmy." He tried to hold her, but she slipped free and ran to that camera, tore it off the tripod and smashed it to the floor.

As she kicked it, crashing it into tiny pieces, she realized that she didn't know why. What part it played in her sister's mystery, she didn't know, but it played some part, she was certain.

Jimmy pulled her away from the camera before she could hurt herself, and finally she collapsed against him.

"Oh, Jimmy, what in the world is going on?"

"I'm taking you home," he whispered. "Come on. Let's go home, and then I'll go back to the bridge."

"No," she cried. "I have to be there. I have to be there when they find her."

Jimmy only nodded his head and helped her out to the car.

The code blue that rang through the hospital summoned every doctor on staff, but Marcus didn't leave Sarah's side as they worked on her. He kept pumping on her heart, his face dripping with the effort and strain of determination, and around him, other doctors, including Gene, who happened to be on duty, called out for life-saving drugs to inject into the IV they had hooked to her arm.

Marcus wouldn't stop pumping, even though there was no longer a heartbeat, and he straddled her and pumped with all his might. Gene worked to hook up the defibrillator, and then they all cleared and tried to shock the heart back to life.

But she didn't stir.

"Again," Marcus demanded, and, following his lead, they tried it again, and then again.

When there was still no heartbeat, Marcus sat back and gaped at her. Gene set his hand on his shoulder. "She's gone, buddy. There's nothing more we can do."

Marcus felt a slow tremor rising up from his heart. She was gone. Only this time she wouldn't be back. This time he couldn't know that she existed in her own time, loving and laughing and living. This time the end was final.

And he couldn't accept it.

He'd brought people back from the dead before, men who had had no chance to live, men whose hearts had thrown in the towel. He had worked them until everyone around him had begged him to stop, until finally he'd gotten a weak, erratic heartbeat. Then, finally... life. He couldn't even count the number of men whose lives would have been discarded if he hadn't been so stubborn.

And Sarah's life was worth more than all of them.

"She's not dead," Marcus said, just as the staff began to turn away. He leaned over her again, began pumping, perspiration dripping from his forehead. "Sarah!" he shouted as he pumped. "Sarah, you're not going to die, damn you! I told you not to come back here, but damn it, you did, and now you're gonna fight with me, because if you don't, if you let go, so help me God, I'll never forgive you!"

Still nothing, but he kept on, until the other doctors were reaching out to stop him, until the nurses looked at him with fear in their eyes, as if he'd snapped right there in their emergency room. But he'd seen those looks before, felt the doubt. It didn't matter to him at all.

Tears stung his eyes as her body jerked with the pressure of his palm against her heart, and he kept pumping, harder and harder, forcing the heart to beat.

"Sarah!" he called. "Sarah, you wake up and look at me! Wake up, Sarah! Damn you, fight this, or none of what has happened is worth anything!"

The bleep on the heart monitor indicated life, and the staff sighed a collective breath of relief and surrounded Sarah again.

"You've got her, Mark," Gene said. "Keep going. I think you're pulling her back."

Marcus kept pumping, his breath coming in gasps, and finally he saw color returning to her face, felt her breathing. He stopped pumping and felt her pulse as it began functioning on its own, and suddenly he wilted, covering his face, and wept from the fear that had driven him to save her.

The room grew quiet, and again, everyone watched him.

"You're a hell of a doctor, Mark Stephens," Gene said finally. "I would have given up long ago."

Marcus tried to pull himself together and shook his head. "You can't give up. Not when there's still hope."

"That's the difference between us," Gene said. "I didn't see any hope there."

Marcus bent over her, touched her face and felt that she was burning with fever. Quickly he looked up and began ordering the drugs that he'd used at home, the ones that had helped her recover before. When all was in motion, he stroked her hair back from her face and was suddenly swept by the overwhelming sensation of grief that he had saved her this time...so that she could experience it again the moment she was called back.

"Why did you do it?" Marcus asked against her cheek. "Why did you come back? It wasn't worth dying over, Sarah."

But Sarah didn't hear from the depths of her coma.

"If you can hear me," he whispered, "pray that Caren doesn't call you back until your heart is stronger. Oh, Sarah, you won't make it again. Baby, you almost didn't make it this time."

He felt the tears streaming down his face and, defeated, he gave in to the grief. But Sarah didn't hear, for she was steeped too deeply in the coma that was holding her hostage. Marcus didn't leave her side for the next several days.

CHAPTER SEVENTEEN

Caren sat on the bank of the river, wrapped in Jimmy's coat, which covered the gown she was still wearing, and watched as the river was dragged in search of her sister's body. She'd never felt so emotionally confused before, she thought as she hugged her knees and watched the progress. With everything they brought up, she watched anxiously, miserably, yet she hoped against all hope that they wouldn't find anything.

Suicide. It didn't feel right. Sarah wasn't the suicidal type. She was an achiever, a dreamer. But she had never been a defeatist.

But maybe those were just the kind who did commit suicide. The kind who put on happy faces and pretended to cope, when inside they were dying, a little at a time.

But wouldn't she have known if her sister felt that way?

Maybe she had known, she told herself as Jimmy left the circle of police and came toward her. Maybe she just hadn't wanted to face it.

She looked up at her husband, her face tear streaked and dirty from the hours sitting out here while the police searched. "What did they say?"

He stooped down next to her and put his arms around her. "They're saying that she might have drifted downriver. That if she's been in there for hours, they're wasting their time dragging here."

Caren's face was dull and expressionless as she nodded. "They're looking so hard," she whispered. "Like they want to find her."

"They do want to, baby," he whispered. "We have to know what happened to her."

"But what if we never find her?" She felt those tears pushing back into her eyes, and she shook her head. "I know this sounds crazy, Jimmy, but I don't feel like she's dead. I feel like something terrible has happened, like she's in some kind of physical danger, but she's still alive."

Jimmy had never doubted the bond the twins had between them, and he only considered Caren's words for a moment. "Well, do you think she's in the river, or maybe on the bank somewhere?"

Caren shook her head. "I feel like this is all a waste of time. I don't think any of this has anything to do with a river. But God only knows what it does have to do with." She burst into tears, and Jimmy held her, but there was nothing he could do to solve this until he could help her discover, once and for all, if Sarah was dead or alive.

Marcus was sitting beside Sarah's bed when she opened her eyes. Immediately he leaned in and stroked her face. "Sarah, wake up. Please wake up."

She managed a weak smile. "Marcus."

Tears came to his eyes, and he pressed a kiss on her cheek. "We almost lost you, baby. You've been out for days."

His eyes looked so tired, so red, and his face was thick with stubble. "Where am I?"

"The hospital. Your heart stopped beating. You were gone, Sarah...."

"But you brought me back." The words were so peaceful, so matter-of-fact, that he almost let them comfort him.

"But I won't be there next time, on the other side. She could call you back anytime, baby. And you won't make it."

Sarah shook her head, and her own eyes welled with tears. "I won't be called back, Marcus," she whispered. "Caren thinks I'm dead."

"What?"

"Suicide," she whispered. "I left a suicide note...." The words exhausted her, and she paused, trying to catch her breath. "She'll think I'm dead."

He stared at her for a long moment, seeing the pain in her eyes, and finally he whispered, "Oh, Sarah...." He held her close, feeling her pain at the separation from her sister, the pain of deception, the pain of inflicting pain on someone she loved.

But suddenly he realized just what it meant to him. It meant that she wouldn't be going home. It meant that she could stay here, living her life with him, loving him for the duration of his days. "Oh, Sarah," he whispered, more intensely now, as an overwhelming sense of rightness washed over him. "Oh, Sarah...."

He laid her back down and looked at her, and she was smiling through her tears. "You're stuck with me now," she whispered.

He closed his eyes against the tears washing down his face, cleansing him of all the tragedy in his life, replacing it with palpable hope. "We're gonna have a good life, Sarah. I promise you that. I'm gonna make you so proud and so happy."

"You already do," she whispered.

And as he held her, she fell asleep in his arms. This time the urgency and anxiety were gone. This time it was okay for her to sleep, for he knew she would wake up, and she would still be here tomorrow.

The clock on the VCR said 3:00 a.m., but Caren still sat curled up on the couch in Jimmy's arms. He was exhausted, she knew, but he wouldn't leave her side. He'd worked as hard today as any of the policemen trying to find Sarah. By sundown, they had all given up.

"She isn't dead," Caren whispered, barely loud enough for Jimmy to hear. "I'd know it."

"Then where is she?" he asked.

Caren shook her head. "I don't know. But she told me to listen to my heart, and, Jimmy, I'm listening, and I still hear her there. She's alive somewhere."

He wiped the tears from her face and sought the words to comfort her. But for the first time since he'd met her, he felt woefully inadequate.

"But I don't feel like she's in trouble anymore," she whispered.

He pulled back from her and looked into her eyes. "What do you feel?"

"Peace," she whispered. "Not mine, but hers. Like she's better. Like she's happy."

Jimmy leaned his head back on the couch and stared out into space, not questioning her words, but not able to feel them, either. "What about you?" he whispered. "If that's all you ever get, just a sensation, just a feeling, will that be enough for you?"

Caren thought for a long moment. "I don't know, Jimmy," she whispered finally as new tears stung her eyes. "I doubt it."

She closed her eyes and thought over all the things that Sarah had told her in the last few months. The common thread of Marcus Stephens seemed to tie things together, yet there was no way to rationalize how it could have.

She thought of the things Sarah had said as she'd hallucinated... things about time travel and being in the right place at the wrong time. Things about finding a soul mate, being in love... Things about Caren always calling her back.

She slipped out of Jimmy's arms and went to the note she had read over a thousand times since Sarah had left it. The first part definitely implied suicide, as if someone else had written it.

But the second part was Sarah, and it was confusing, as if there was some secret message there. Something that she meant for Caren to absorb rather than read.

Caren, please don't grieve for me. When you despair, listen to your heart. The same heart that told you when I hurt myself as a child, the same heart that helps you read my mind sometimes, whether I want you to or not. Your heart will know the truth, and you can trust it. Your heart will tell you how much better off I am. Remember the things I've told you.

The things she'd told her. She thought of the crazy things Sarah had said while hallucinating, things she had discounted and ignored. But they were impossible, weren't they?

Still, her heart told her of peace and happiness and hope, and that was so much better than grief and despair and death. She held the note close to her heart and cried some more. But finally, with that tiny cloud of hope dimming the pain, she fell asleep in her husband's arms.

The sky shone brightly on the day that Marcus took Sarah home from the hospital, and though she was still weak, the smile in her eyes was stronger than any illness could be. She smiled over at him as he drove, and she took his hand.

"I have two surprises for you," he said, bringing her hand to his lips.

"What?" she asked, delighted.

"The first one," he said, "is that the chief of staff of the hospital approached me yesterday, trying to convince me to come back to work. They need good surgeons, apparently, and he's not convinced that I've lost it."

"You're a legend," she said. "The nurses told me that they'd never seen anyone fight so long and hard to save anyone. They need more doctors like you, Marcus."

"I know," he said. "And the truth is, it hit me while I was working on you how many lives I've been able to save. I kept remembering their faces, their wounds, their hopelessness. But they're walking around today. I focused on that while I was working on you, and I told myself that if I'd saved them, I would save you."

"And you did."

"By God's grace, I did. And anyone else there would have let you die. I guess I realized then that I belonged in medicine. And from now on, I'll count the lives saved, instead of the ones lost. I'll count the successes, instead of the mistakes."

"So you're going back to work?"

He smiled. "As soon as you have your strength back, I'll have a place at the hospital."

She leaned across the seat and threw her arms around him. "Oh, Marcus, that's wonderful. I'm so proud of you. It wasn't fair, your tormenting yourself for nothing. Blocking yourself off from everything you love because you made a mistake."

His smile faded, and he leaned his head on hers as he drove. "I won't forget, though, Sarah. I'll never forget that."

"I know," she whispered. "There will be a sad place for that in your heart, and it probably won't ever go away. Just like the sad place I had for you when you ran out in front of that car. But it's gone now, because you're here with me. And by saving me, you've redeemed yourself for that child. I believe that, Marcus.''

Pensive, they leaned against each other for a long moment, quiet as they savored the sadness they had both embraced in their lives. But then Sarah tucked it into its place and found her smile again. ''What's the second surprise?''

His smile was mischievous as he spoke. ''I've been busy, when I wasn't with you in the hospital. I've been taking care of getting you legal. I pulled some strings, albeit illegal ones, to get you a birth certificate so that you could live a normal life here. And I've been buying you some clothes, preparing the house... And there's one dress that I thought would be so beautiful on you. I thought you could wear it... to the wedding.''

''Wedding?'' Her eyes were misty as she gazed up at him. ''What wedding?''

''The one that's going to take place at Holy Cross this very afternoon. Brother Bobby's going to meet us there, if that's all right with you.''

She caught her breath on a sob and threw her arms around him again.

And that was all the answer Marcus needed.

Multicolored rays of sunlight filtered through the stained-glass window like a benediction from God as the preacher pronounced them man and wife. Marcus kissed his bride—it was surely the sweetest, most tender, most poignant kiss any groom had ever of-

fered—as the preacher looked on with a smile. But it
was impossible for him to understand the significance
of that kiss, or the marriage of these souls, for their
union was a defiance of time, a rebellion against human reality.

Marcus's eyes were misty as he broke the kiss. He
kept his forehead pressed against hers and stroked her
face with an adoring hand. "Thank you for giving me
a reason to start living again," he whispered. "I know
now that you weren't my punishment, but a sweet,
precious gift that I could never deserve as long as I
live. But that doesn't mean I won't try to."

Tears streamed down her face, scoring her happiness, and she stood on tiptoe and kissed him again.

He pulled her by the hand out the door, and, waving goodbye to the pastor, they drove up to the bridge,
parked the car and got out. The river looked peaceful
and slow today as they leaned on the rail, and Sarah
whispered, "I can't believe I don't have to go back.
That I can stay and be your wife, and take care of
you...."

"Make a wish," he said, slipping his arms around
her from behind. "Throw the bouquet and make a
wish."

"Will that work?" she teased.

Marcus smiled. "For us it will. Heaven and earth
have moved for us, and time has gone in reverse. Go
ahead," he whispered again. "Make any wish you
want."

Sarah closed her eyes and buried her face in the
spray of flowers she held in her hand. Despite the urgency of her desire to hold on to the happiness Mar-

cus had given her today, she couldn't keep her mind from drifting to Caren and her broken heart, her sad spirit. "I wish for peace for Caren," she said. "And some kind of understanding, so she'll know it's all right."

"Then I wish that, too," Marcus whispered.

She threw the bouquet, watched it fall to the water, then drift downstream, slowly, perfectly, as if it knew exactly where to carry her wish.

Then together, they got back into the car and drove to the home they would share for years to come, where they would raise children of their own as Marcus practiced medicine and Sarah took pictures of all the simplicity and beauty she saw around her, so that one day, somewhere in the nineties, someone who cared might pick up the collection and know what it had been like.

They consummated their marriage, taking their slow, sweet time, and the promise of a future in the same place at the same time gave it a newer, sweeter dimension than they'd shared before. Gone was the urgency, the despair, the tragedy, and now they felt delirium that lingered, ecstasy that held on, and satisfaction that didn't threaten to disappear with the call of a name.

That night, Sarah fell asleep in her husband's arms, knowing she'd still be there when she awoke, that soon they would be thinking not about time travel and separation and sickness, but about groceries and bills and all the mundane things that husbands and wives thought of. Only they would never be mundane, she thought, for they had worked too hard to have what they had. Neither of them would ever be taken for granted.

In her heart, Sarah felt a sweet peace for the sacrifices she'd had to make to be his wife. Already she felt that Caren was all right, that somewhere through the grief and confusion she'd allowed Sarah's truths to filter down.

She must feel Sarah's happiness, she thought, for it was greater than any pain or heartache or fear that Caren had sensed in her before. Caren would know, she thought with a smile.

Somehow, Caren would know.

CHAPTER EIGHTEEN

Marcus Stephens was the key, Caren thought as the light of dawn invaded her living room, where she still lay entangled in her husband's arms. She needed to know more about him. She needed to find whatever Sarah had found that had obsessed her so. Maybe then, somehow, she'd be able to find her sister.

She got up and showered, and when she came out, Jimmy was on the phone with the police department. There was still no news, he told her, but they would be resuming their search in an hour or so.

She went into the kitchen, where Jimmy was hanging up the phone, and pressed a kiss on his tired face. "I'm going out for a while."

"Where?" he asked.

"I don't know," she said. "Just...I need to get out...to think."

"Then I'm coming with you."

"No," she said. "I need to do some things. Just to work them out in my mind. You won't understand."

He put his arms around her. His big frame dwarfed her, but made her feel protected at the same time. "You're exhausted, sweetheart, and you're overwrought. You don't have to explain anything to me, and I'll be quiet and let you think. But I'm not leaving your side today."

Quietly she acquiesced, and he quickly showered and dressed. When they got in the car, he kept his word and let her drive.

The thing was, she didn't know where she wanted to go. But she had to find out about Marcus Stephens.

His landlady, she thought. There had been a landlady, who had given Sarah his things. Maybe, if she could speak to her, she could find out some more. Maybe something she said would give Caren some idea that could unravel this mystery.

"I have to make a phone call," she told Jimmy. "I have to call Marcus Stephens's landlady."

He shot her a strange look, and even though he didn't question her, she took his hand. "I don't know why, Jimmy. It just seems like something I need to do."

"Hey, I'm not questioning you," he whispered. "Your intuitive powers where Sarah's concerned are something I've never tried to understand. They just are. Do whatever you have to do, baby."

She got out of the car and looked up Marcus Stephens's phone number, still listed in the phone book that had come out before his death. She dialed the number, fully expecting a disconnect recording, but a woman answered.

"Hello?"

"Uh . . . yes." She cleared her throat. "My name is Caren Allen. You don't know me, but I was wondering if I might come by and speak to you. About Marcus Stephens."

"Well . . . yes, I'd be happy to speak to you," the woman said. She gave her the address, and Caren jotted it down on the corner of the phone book's cover, then tore it off. "Thank you. I'll be right over."

She got back into the car and looked at her husband. "We're going to see Marcus Stephens's landlady," she said.

He nodded. "All right."

They drove quietly to the address the woman had given her and pulled into the drive of a big, beautiful old house trimmed with flowers that hung from window boxes and sprouted from the garden in front in every shape and size. The scent of happiness and joy wafted on the air, and Caren turned confused eyes on her husband. "It's beautiful. I wonder why Sarah didn't mention it. She loves houses like this, and she would have loved the flowers. . . ."

Shrugging, Jimmy got out of the car, and Caren followed. Hand in hand, they slowly walked to the door.

The woman who answered smiled at them at once. "Hello, there. You must be Caren."

"Yes," she said. "I hope I'm not interrupting anything. I know this was short notice, but I'd like to talk to you about Marcus Stephens. My sister told me he had boarded here."

"Boarded here?" The woman threw her head back and laughed. "Oh, my, no. Dr. Stephens lives here, all right, but he owns this house. I'm just the housekeeper."

"Housekeeper?" Caren glanced at Jimmy.

"Did you say he *lives* here?" Jimmy asked. "Maybe we've got the wrong house. We're looking for Marcus Stephens, who died after being hit by a car a few months ago."

The housekeeper's smile faded. "Well, it must be another Marcus Stephens. As old as he is, this one's definitely alive. As a matter of fact, you can talk to him yourself if you want. He and his wife are down at the park. They like to go this time of day and feed the birds."

Caren's frown seemed etched into her forehead as she looked in the direction of the park. "Well...maybe we'll do that. Do you think they'll mind?"

"Mind? Heavens, no. Dr. Mark and Sarah love young people. Go right ahead."

"Sarah?" Caren caught her breath, and her heart began to hammer in her ears with life-threatening force. She felt Jimmy's arm closing over her shoulders, felt him turning her around, heard him thanking the woman for her help.

He got her into the car and set her down on the passenger's seat. For a moment, they only stared. "This is weird," Jimmy said.

Caren shook her head. "You have no idea how weird."

Jimmy sucked in a deep breath. "It must be a different man, that's all. And it's just a coincidence...."

"Maybe," Caren whispered. "Maybe not."

He started the car and drove her to the park, and from the street she saw the backs of an old couple hunched together on a bench, throwing popcorn out to a flock of birds. They laughed as the birds fluttered overhead, waving up and down as popcorn was thrown.

"Stay here," Caren whispered. "I have to do this myself."

Jimmy didn't argue as Caren got out of the car and walked slowly across the park. Her heart hammered as she approached the couple, her hands trembled, and she found herself unable to breathe. Sarah's voice that day in the hospital raged through her mind, over and over, as she drew closer.

You always call me back, Caren.... Next time, don't call me back. Just let me go and know that I belong there... with him....

Tears flowed down her face, and suddenly the old woman stood up. Caren stopped.

She watched as the woman turned around, and from behind a pair of wire-rimmed glasses her eyes met Caren's.

Sarah, Caren thought. It's Sarah. But she was old. As Caren beheld her sister, with gray hair, wrinkles withering her skin, her backbone slightly stooped, she saw the joy in her eyes, and the recognition, the emotion. And, suddenly, the fear.

Don't call me back.... Please don't call me back....

Caren fought the urge to run forward, embrace Sarah, hold her and cry over her. But the very fear and apprehension in the old woman's eyes kept her from it.

Something deep within the recesses of her heart told her that it wouldn't work. What Sarah had told her, what she'd discounted as insanity and ignored as madness, had happened.

Sarah hadn't been dreaming when she'd told her of time travel and a man who loved her and her need to be there with him. And she hadn't been imagining when she'd begged Caren not to undo what had been done.

And if it was true, she realized, just approaching her sister could throw the whole process into reverse. It could wipe away an entire lifetime. It could invalidate all the joy she saw in her sister's eyes.

Slowly, Caren backed away.

As she did she saw the emotion twisting Sarah's old face, the tears slowly rolling down her cheeks, the memories misting in her eyes. The old man stood up, and he, too, looked at Caren, as though he recognized her, as though he feared her....

I won't call you back, Caren wept out in her mind, and somehow she knew that Sarah heard. Slowly she backed farther away.

Sarah watched her, not looking away, and finally Caren turned her back to the couple, and her walk grew more rapid, more urgent, until she was running back to her car.

Jimmy waited with worried, compassionate eyes. "Did you talk to them?"

"No," she whispered.

"Well...I thought you were going to ask them about Sarah...."

"I didn't have to," she said. She leaned her head back on the headrest and gave in to the tears crowding through her. She watched as the old man seemed to console the woman, tenderly stroking her back as they made their way out of the park.

When they were gone, she turned her tear-streaked face to Jimmy. "Sarah's not dead. She's happy, Jimmy. And she's having a good life."

"Where?" he asked.

She drew in a deep breath and thought of telling him, but this was something she needed to keep for herself. Something just between her and her beloved twin sister. Something she could always hold close, instead of her sister.

"Somewhere," she whispered. "Somewhen."

He gazed at her in confusion for a moment, then took her hand, accepting the explanation without question.

"Let's go," she whispered.

"Do you want to go back to the river?" he asked. "They're still looking for her."

A soft smile touched Caren's lips. "No. They won't find her there."

She scooted closer to her husband, laid her head on his shoulder. "Let's go home," she whispered. "Sarah's gonna be all right."

As they pulled away, Caren saw the old couple walking home on the sidewalk ahead of them. Caren set her hand on Jimmy's leg. "Slow down," she whispered.

The car slowed next to the old man and woman, and Caren caught Sarah's eyes through the window.

Sarah blinked back tears as she brought her arthritic hand to her mouth, pressed a kiss on it and blew it to Caren.

Caren smiled and reached up, pretending to catch it. Then, closing her hand in a tight fist, she held it to her heart as she and Jimmy left the old couple behind.

* * * * *

And now from Silhouette Shadows
an exciting preview of

BREAK THE NIGHT
by Anne Stuart

PROLOGUE

The sky over Los Angeles was bloodred.

At first they thought it was a new form of toxic waste. Red smog, caused by a combination of industrial exhaust and the peculiar weather conditions. A good stiff wind would blow everything away in just a matter of time.

But the red sky continued, and the scientists began to debate. It had to be caused by the latest nuclear accident, perhaps, or brushfires burning out of control. Maybe even an act of God.

The historians were no comfort. The red sky had been recorded throughout the past, from France in the 1400s, when Gilles de Retz swathed a bloody path through the countryside, to London in the fall of 1888, when Jack the Ripper made his rounds, to Germany in 1905, when Peter Kurten, the Düsseldorf Ripper, carved his way through a terrified populace.

The Santa Ana winds blew hot and dry from the desert, swirling down from the bloodred sky, and suicide rates tripled. The endless storms followed, drenching the sprawling cityscape. And somewhere in the dark, rain-soaked streets of Venice, California, Springheeled Jack, Saucy Jack, Jack the Ripper, made one of his periodic reappearances. And the streets ran red with blood, so much blood that not even the rain could wash them clean.

CHAPTER ONE

Lizzie Stride pushed her hair away from her face, leaving a streak of red paint across her high cheekbone. It was too hot in her studio apartment, but she couldn't afford to turn up the air-conditioning. She couldn't open any window, either—the rain had been falling nonstop for days now, and even her skin felt moldy. Running the dehumidifier already ate up about half her electricity allowance—she couldn't afford to crank up the air conditioner besides.

As long as her work survived, she could sit there and suffer. No one melted from a little heat and humidity, even if it felt as if she might. What mattered was the mask beneath her hands, as she smoothed and shaped the red-tinged clay over the heavy eyebrows. If anything, the weather was good for it, keeping the material pliant for a longer stretch of time. Long enough for her to decide exactly how she wanted to shape this one. How to perfect it.

She took several deep, calming breaths. Surely she could lower her steamy body temperature by meditating. The mind was infinitely powerful—she just hadn't learned how to harness hers. She could hear Kate Bush on the radio, singing something eerie, a fitting counterpoint to the face beneath her fingertips. It had turned evil beneath her hands, as her masks had done far too often of late. She didn't tend to waste much time analyzing her work. Each face grew on its own beneath her long, deft fingers. Sometimes a clown, made of garish colors and absurd features, sometimes a diva with ostrich feathers and jewels. And sometimes a fiend from hell.

Unfortunately, the monsters sold better than the other, more frivolous, masks. It was no wonder, she thought, shoving her hair back again. The world was full of human monsters, and LA had more than its share.

They'd found the sixth body two days ago in a Dumpster in Venice, and within hours she'd been trapped at the police station once more, trying to make sense of random savagery that should have had no connection to her at all. Except for the fact that each victim was wearing one of her masks when the body was found.

The Venice Ripper, they were calling him. Fortunately the newspapers didn't know about the masks, or about the truly horrifying details of the medically accurate butchery of the prostitute victims. Lizzie was still anonymous enough, an innocent pulled into the horror by her art and a madman's random appreciation.

When the police had traced the second mask to her, she'd stopped working for a while—too horrified by the piece of evidence she'd identified. The blood-soaked papier-mâché had once been a Kewpie doll face, and the knowledge that the killer had used her masks during his bizarre killing spree made her feel sick inside, like an unwilling accessory to a madman.

But stopping her work, hiding in her apartment when she wasn't making ends meet as a waitress at the Pink Pelican Café, did no good at all. She'd made a lot of masks in the two years she'd been in the Los Angeles area. Sold a fair number. And the killer seemed to have an inexhaustible supply.

She sat back, staring at the mask beneath her fingers. The red streaks looked like blood, the mouth was open in a silent hideous scream, and somewhere a killer waited. One of her masks in his murderous hands.

Kate Bush stopped singing. The news came on, a muffled voice, one she didn't want to hear. The Ripper had claimed another victim, the body found dumped behind a building near the beach.

And Lizzie brought her fists down on the mask, crushing it beneath her strong hands.

Damien stood in the window overlooking the gray, endless city, his long fingers gripped tightly around the mug of coffee. He'd lost weight in the past couple of months, more than was good for him. And it was no wonder—he subsisted on a diet of black coffee, straight tequila, cigarettes and fast food. That was, when he remembered to eat. Most of the time he forgot.

It was all right, though. He'd grown soft in the past few years. Life could do that to you. Too many awards, too much money, and things got a little too easy.

Not that they were easy for him now. He'd left his job at the *Chronicle* after the second Ripper murder. After the second nightmare. Left his Pulitzer and his retirement fund and his beautiful, intelligent research assistant who'd let him know she was interested in doing more than his legwork, left behind the toughest, fairest editor in the business. Left behind a weekly paycheck and his only connection to sanity.

None of that mattered. None of the safe, comfortable things he'd worked for made any difference to him any longer. He was a man possessed, driven, with only one need in life. To find the Ripper. And stop him.

He looked at his reflection in the rain-streaked window. The gaunt, unshaven cheeks, dark, tormented eyes, his hair long and shaggy. The Ripper probably looked a great deal like him. Haunted. Hunted. Driven.

Damien leaned his forehead against the grimy window, staring out into the bleak twilight before he shut his eyes. Only to see the blood once more, and hear the scream of the dying woman. The sound that would live in his mind forever. And he smashed his forehead against the glass, once, twice, until he heard the window crack.

The apartment was still and silent hours later when Lizzie let herself back in, locking the door behind her. She'd turned off the air-conditioning before she left, and the accumulated heat and dampness swept over her like a wave. She leaned against the door, not bothering to turn on the light. She could smell the clay from the smashed mask, the bitter oily odor from that morning's coffee, mixed with the memory of yesterday's pasta. She could almost wish for the hot dry desert winds to sweep through, clearing away the constant, heavy rain.

"We'll be glad to give you police protection," Detective Finlay Adamson, the middle-aged, coffee-guzzling, avuncular police lieutenant working on the Ripper case had told Lizzie when he drove her back to her apartment late that afternoon. This time they'd only kept her three hours, going over the same old unanswerable questions. "I don't think you're in any particular danger—this psycho only goes for prostitutes, and he'd have no reason to hurt you. For what it's worth, the police psychiatrist thinks he considers you some kind of ally, and..."

"Please, don't!" Lizzie begged, the nausea rising. "It's not my fault that some monster uses my masks."

"Calm down, Miss Stride. No one's blaming you," Adamson said in his patient voice.

"But can't you see I'm blaming myself? As far as I know, no one's bought more than two or three masks of mine. I've asked everyone who sells them for me, and no one remembers making any more sales than that. Are you certain you've checked all the galleries and gift shops...?"

"You wouldn't believe how many times we've checked," Adamson said wearily. "The kind of place that carries your stuff isn't great on keeping records. We're just lucky we found you in the first place. A reporter happened to recognize one of the murder masks as yours. Apparently he has a couple of them himself."

The sick feeling in Lizzie's stomach didn't subside. "A reporter who collects masks? Who's covering the Ripper murders? Doesn't that strike you as a little too coincidental? Are you sure . . . ?"

"Don't do my job for me, Miss Stride. Everyone's a suspect in this case, even the most unlikely people. Including yourself. We haven't discounted Damien, even if it doesn't seem possible."

"Damien?"

"Used to write for the *Chronicle*. J. R. Damien. He quit a few months ago to concentrate on the Ripper murders. Apparently he's writing a book about them. Still does all their coverage of the case. So far, he's cooperated and kept quiet about the masks." Adamson's tone of voice made it clear what he thought of such ghoulish behavior. "Now, don't go getting paranoid about all this. We think the Ripper's got enough masks to keep him busy for quite a while—you said that last one you sold more than a year ago, so he must have been planning this for a while. Just keep your doors locked and your guard up."

"I do anyway. This is Southern California, remember?" Lizzie said with a delicate little shudder.

"How could I forget?" Adamson said. "Give us a call if anything seems unusual."

Lizzie stared around her dimly lit apartment for a moment, willing herself not to imagine murderous shadows where none existed. She shouldn't have been so quick to turn down police protection. She shouldn't have been so quick to take Adamson's word for it that she was safe.

She flicked on the light, kicking off her sandals and crossing the rough wood floor to stare at her ruined mask. She *was* safe, she reminded herself. No one knew who she was, presumably not even the Ripper. He simply had an affinity for her masks.

She shivered at the horrible thought, moving on into the kitchen area of the small, spare apartment and reaching for a bottle of fruit juice. She needed to get away from here. If only she had family, money, some kind of escape.

Her family was long gone, her father no more than a name on a birth certificate, her mother dead by the time Lizzie was in college. As for money, that had always been a scarce commodity, and working as a craftsperson in an overpopulated area like LA didn't lend itself to financial solvency.

Her friends, mostly actors, writers and the like, were even more impoverished than she was. None of them could lend her the money to get out of town, to go someplace where the sun could shine without murderous winds ripping through her hair, a place where she could breathe, where she could meet a stranger's gaze and not have to worry about whether he was going to hit on her. Or cut her throat.

No, for now she was trapped in her heat-soaked apartment. At least no one connected her with the Ripper murders. No one besides the police and that one reporter even knew about the masks.

Except, of course, the Ripper.

SILHOUETTE® *Shadows*™

Welcome To The Dark Side Of Love...

AVAILABLE THIS MONTH

#7 FLASHBACK—Terri Herrington

An antique camera, an elderly gentleman and a Victorian house altered photographer Sarah Rhinehart's life forever. With every click of the shutter, she traveled back in time—and discovered love. But would such forbidden passion come only at the cost of her life?

#8 WAITING FOR THE WOLF MOON—Evelyn Vaughn

When newcomer Rand Garner showed up in town, he had Sylvia Peabody's heart pumping with desire—and her mind racing with fear. With full-moon murders and rumors of werewolves rife, she wondered, could the charming man with the wolfish grin really be a carnivorous canine?

COMING NEXT MONTH

#9 BREAK THE NIGHT—Anne Stuart

A face behind every mask—a mask behind every murder. Lizzie Stride was up to her pretty little neck in trouble. Someone was using her masks in a rash of murders. And journalist J. R. Damien, the only person willing to protect her, might be the killer. Was he reporting the news... or creating it?

#10 IMMINENT THUNDER—Rachel Lee

Honor Nightingale moved to the Florida coast dreaming of sunny days and beautiful beaches. Instead she found terror. And the only person she could turn to was Ian McLaren, a man she didn't trust. With the finger of evil pointing to Ian, Honor wondered if this sexy man was as sinful as he looked....

A romantic collection that
will touch your heart....

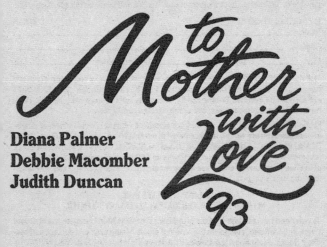

Diana Palmer
Debbie Macomber
Judith Duncan

**As part of your annual tribute to
motherhood, join three of Silhouette's
best-loved authors as they celebrate the
joy of one of our most precious gifts—
mothers.**

Available in May at your favorite retail outlet.

Only from  *Silhouette*®

—where passion lives.

SHADOWS FREE GIFT OFFER

To receive your free gift, send us three proofs-of-purchase from any Silhouette Shadows™ books from March, April or May with the Free Gift Certificate properly completed, plus a check or money order (do not send cash) for $2.25 to cover postage and handling, payable to Silhouette Shadows Promotion Offer. We will send you the specified gift.

FREE GIFT CERTIFICATE   096 KAN

Name: _____

Address: _____

City: _____ State/Prov: _____ Zip/Postal Code: _____

Mail this certificate, three proofs-of-purchase and check or money order for postage and handling to: Silhouette Shadows Promotion, P.O. Box 9071, Buffalo, NY 14269-9071 or P.O. Box 604, Fort Erie, Ontario L2A 5X3. Requests must be received by June 30, 1993. No liability is assumed for lost, late or misdirected certificates.

PLUS—Every time you submit a completed certificate with the correct number of proofs-of-purchase, you are automatically entered in our HAUNTING SWEEPSTAKES to win the GRAND PRIZE OF A THREE-DAY TOUR OF SALEM, MASSACHUSETTS, for two, including accommodation, airfare, sightseeing tours and $500 spending money. No purchase or obligation necessary to enter. See below for alternate means of entry and how to obtain complete sweepstakes rules.

HAUNTING SWEEPSTAKES
NO PURCHASE OR OBLIGATION NECESSARY TO ENTER

To enter and take advantage of the SHADOWS Free Gift Offer, complete and mail your Free Gift Certificate, along with the required proofs-of-purchase and postage and handling charge, to: Silhouette Shadows Promotion, P.O. Box 9071, Buffalo, NY 14269-9071 or P.O. Box 604, Fort Erie, Ontario L2A 5X3. ALTERNATIVELY, you may enter the sweepstakes without taking advantage of the SHADOWS gift offer, by hand-printing on a 3" × 5" card (mechanical reproductions are not acceptable) your name and address and mailing it to: Haunting Sweepstakes, P.O. Box 9069, Buffalo, NY 14269-9069 or P.O. Box 626, Fort Erie, Ontario L2A 5X3. Limit: one entry per envelope. Entries must be sent via First Class mail and be received no later than June 30, 1993. No liability is assumed for lost, late or misdirected mail.

Sweepstakes is open to residents of the U.S. (except Puerto Rico) and Canada, 21 years of age or older. For complete rules, send a self-addressed, stamped envelope (WA residents need not affix return postage) to: Haunting Sweepstakes Rules, P.O. Box 4682, Blair, NE 68009

To collect your free necklace you must include the necessary proofs-of-purchase with a properly completed offer certificate.

ONE PROOF-OF-PURCHASE

096 KAN